C000063297

Copyright © 2022 by Holly Annaleisha

Photography: Brunoworks, Shutterstock

Cover Design: BooksnMoods

Contents

Prologue

THE BEGINNING

TWELVE YEARS AGO

JAKE CREMELL WAS DESTINED for failure, or at least, that's what Sarah Colling's mother constantly told her.

'I can't believe you just did that,' Sarah said. 'Mr. Carol is so going to call your mum.'

'Like my mum is even home right now.' Jake smirked. 'It's past twelve on a Friday, and her dole money came in this morning. So she'll be down at The Blue Bell getting trashed as we speak.'

Growing up in Baynor Green was never easy. It was a small town with a clear divide between its poorer and wealthier parts. They did, however, share the same schools, restaurants, pubs, and supermarkets. Sarah was grateful to have been brought up on the wealthier side. Her father was a well-respected doctor, and her mother was a socialite. This gave Sarah a helping hand in becoming one of the most popular girls in school. Her peers often told her she was gorgeous, with her long dark hair, blue-green

1

eyes, and expensive clothes. She was the trendiest teenager in town. Her mother made sure of that.

Jake was from the 'wrong side of town,' as her parents would say. He was blond, tall, and slim, with a few pimples on his forehead like most sixteen-year-olds. What captivated Sarah about Jake were his piercing green eyes. They had a cheeky sparkle in them, reflecting his profound confidence.

'Well, you know how Mr. Carol is. He'll never forget this. Showing him up in front of the entire class.' Sarah snorted.

Sarah and Jake had known each other since they were four years old. They first met in the nursery school playground, when he pushed her off the swing set and declared that 'yucky' girls were not welcome. Sarah was a tiny child with a pixie haircut, which had earned her the dreaded 'pixie' nickname, a name she couldn't shake even after growing out her dark hair to the point where it almost touched her waist.

They got 'married' under the slides at the local park when they were six, with only Sarah's twin brother, Ryker, and her best friend, Brooke, in attendance. It had been a great day until Ryker ate the Haribo wedding ring and ran away laughing. Jake broke Sarah's crayon in class two weeks later, and they 'divorced.'

Sarah had gotten into trouble for the first time at the age of nine, when she pulled Missy Smith's hair in the middle of class—all because Missy had asked Jake to be her boyfriend.

When they were eleven, Sarah and Jake shared their first kiss behind the large tree in the corner of the school field. Jake asked Sarah to be his girlfriend on her twelfth birthday, which fell on the first week of year seven. Even at such a young age, they both knew that many people in their lives would not approve, due to their different backgrounds. Sarah was reminded of this daily by her image-obsessed mother, who sneered and cursed under her breath whenever they encountered anyone from Jake's side of town. It took years for her mother to accept Ryker and Jake's friendship. So Sarah couldn't imagine how she'd react if she found out her daughter was dating him.

As a result, they kept their relationship a secret for the first two years of high school, relying on notes passed back and forth in class or secretive smiles exchanged whenever they passed each other in the hallway. Then they'd try to meet up as much as they could in their secret location: behind an oak tree in a run-down park near Jake's house.

Jake sent her a slightly different message when they were fourteen. This one was a little more elaborate and risky. He asked Sarah if she wanted to meet him after school at the bike sheds and go for a public stroll around town. After weighing her options and considering the potential backlash, she agreed. She knew it would cause an uproar, particularly with her mum, but it was a risk she was willing to take if it meant being with Jake in public.

They became inseparable from that day on, both inside and outside school. Their respective circles of friends couldn't understand what they saw in each other at first. Sarah's friends didn't quite understand what she saw in 'scruffy Jake from the council estate,' as they dubbed him. Jake's friends—who spent most of their time trashing the local park and stealing from the corner shop—wondered what it was about the 'triple S'—short for 'swotty, stuck-up Sarah'—that piqued Jake's interest, but neither of them cared what anyone else thought.

None of their friends understood their relationship or how alive and loved Jake made Sarah feel. They didn't know about the love notes he'd leave in her schoolbag every morning when they met before school, or how he'd squared up to Billy Newman, the most brutal lad in school, when he called her a stuck-up bitch.

As expected, her mother became even more domineering than before and barred Jake from entering the house. She demanded that Sarah end her relationship with him right away, which Sarah of course refused to do. This was the beginning of months' worth of arguing that Sarah could have done without. The only friend she had who accepted their relationship was Brooke.

Brooke, who was slightly larger than the other girls in their class, didn't fit in with Sarah's group of friends. They saw her as Sarah's 'sidekick' or 'tag along,' but Brooke was tough. She gave as good as she got without taking any prisoners, and Sarah loved her for it.

Ryker, Sarah's twin brother, was the black sheep of the Colling family, the troublemaker who was a nightmare to control, especially for teachers and other authority figures. Even though Sarah and Ryker were twins, they were nothing alike; if it weren't for their eyes and last name, you'd never guess they were related. Brooke despised him vehemently. Most people didn't blame her, though, as he was the one who gave her the nickname 'Brookie Cookie' and persuaded most of the lads in their year to do the same.

While Ryker was the bad seed, their older brother Dylan, whom Ryker referred to as the 'Golden Boy,' was their rock, the peacemaker, and the one person who kept everyone in their household in line. Without Dylan, their entire family would have fallen apart years ago. It was a lot of pressure to put on her brother's head, but when their father would leave for his frequent business trips, it was Dylan who looked after them, despite what her mother said. Dylan was about to leave for university soon, which Sarah knew would put a strain on the entire family.

'Why don't we skip school and go to your house instead? Your dad's still at the surgery, isn't he?' Jake said with a sly grin.

'I can't miss school. Our final English exam is tomorrow. My dad will lose his shit if I don't get at least a B. So you can forget about skipping when we're supposed to be revising.' Sarah sighed.

'Fine, whatever you say,' Jake said, rolling his eyes as he pulled out a pack of Marlboros from his gym bag.

'What are you doing?' Sarah snapped. 'Put them away before a teacher sees you. We're in the school corridor, and you don't want Mr. Carol to have any more leverage against you.' She grabbed his pack of cigarettes and shoved them back into his duffel.

'Fine, sweetheart, but I'm only doing it for you.'

Sarah had planned her entire future around Jake because she knew they would be together forever, or so she thought at the time, but when you're sixteen, forever is a short time, and you quickly realise life isn't the fairy tale you imagined it to be.

· · · ● · ● · ● · · ·

SIX YEARS AGO

'WASN'T THIS WHAT YOU wanted? For us to be together and have a family? I thought you were in love with me.' Britney Adamson murmured, her gaze fixed on the specks of dirt scattered across the floor. Her long blond hair fell messily down her shoulders, and her light brown eyes filled to the brim with tears as she tried to avoid his gaze. Britney had hoped that things would be different, that she had finally found someone to rescue her and take her away from this place. Even though she had foolishly gotten involved with him while he was still with his girlfriend, he promised Britney when they first met that he was leaving her.

Britney first met Ian on a Sunday afternoon at Bevington Market. Her neighbour had told her that some of the best clothing knockoffs were being sold at half price and, with her wage, she was going to take what she could get.

Britney was struck right away by Ian's size. He could cast a shadow that would fill a large market stall. He was stocky, with tanned skin, light-blue eyes, and black hair that looked like it had a streak of blue in the right light. Britney had noticed Ian before; how could she not? He was gorgeous. She never had the guts to talk to him, though, considering who he was—and who she was. Britney Adamson, daughter of the town bike and father unknown. Well, probably unknown; she did once hear that it was a toss-up between Mr. Bryce, their local shop owner, and some guy called Josh who left town straight after he left school. Her mum gave birth to her when she was sixteen. She was kicked out of her house by Britney's grandad soon after and hadn't been back since. She signed on for unemployment benefits and housing assistance as soon as she could and got herself and her daughter a two-bedroom council flat. It was a speedy process, a lot quicker than it would be nowadays, her mum claimed.

Over the years, men had come in and out of their lives, sometimes so quickly that Britney didn't even remember their names, or maybe she was never even told them. Her mum had an 'out of sight, out of mind' policy. Britney could disappear for a week and her mum wouldn't even bat an eyelid; well, not until an educational welfare officer showed up at their flat asking questions. Then she would send Britney straight back to school because nothing would be worse for her than losing the child benefit, which paid for her weekly piss-up.

Ian spotted Britney across that market that day and came over to introduce himself. At first, Britney thought he was taking the piss. He was so sweet, charming, and attentive. No one had paid her such attention before, least of all someone from the nice part of town. They had an instant connection, or so she thought at the time. He asked for her number and she gave it to him, which was the start of their relationship.

He told her that same week that he had a girlfriend, Sarah, whom he was in the process of leaving because he'd recently found out she'd cheated on him. Britney had heard about his girlfriend before, but she didn't know her. They didn't run in the same circles.

Ian and Britney met up a lot over those next few weeks. He took her on several out-of-town dates to nice restaurants, bought her nice clothes, and made her feel like a million pounds. Britney had thought she had finally found someone with whom she could build a life, someone who could get her out of the estate that, over the years, she'd convinced herself she was destined to die in. After about a month of dating, she finally brought up the subject of Sarah again, but he waved the question off. Britney naïvely assumed that meant he had broken up with Sarah and was fully committed to her.

Ian would always have Britney meet him at his friend Tony's house; his ex-girlfriend owned the apartment he used to share with her, so he was between places at the time, or so Britney thought. Then, after about six months, he told her he was in love with her and wanted them to get a place together. Britney was ecstatic. He wanted to leave it for a while, though; he claimed he was due this big promotion at work, and he wanted it to go through before they looked into anything.

A couple of weeks later, she missed her period and took herself to the local pharmacy to buy a pregnancy test. Surprise, she was pregnant.

'I don't want a kid yet, especially not one with you,' he sneered.

'What do you mean, "especially not with me?"' she mumbled, distraught, as she stared at the same spot on the floor.

'Honestly, how naïve are you? Look, we can sort this out today. Get rid of it, and we will pick up where we left off.'

'I... I want to keep it.'

'Keep it? You stupid bitch, do you really think I want the embarrassment of calling you my child's mother, knowing who you are and where you come from? The town slag Melanie Adamson's daughter from the dirtiest flat on the estate. You're a tramp. Why do you think I've been keeping things on the down low between us? Because all you were meant to be was a bit of fun.' He chuckled darkly.

Britney felt her chest collapse; she took a few deep breaths to ensure her body was still functioning and that she hadn't died inside.

'You told me you loved me! We were going to get an apartment together once you got your big promotion. We were going to build a life together!' she sobbed as she glanced up at him, no longer able to hold her tears in as they slowly fell down her cheeks.

At that moment, part of Britney wondered if this was inevitable. Was she born to live and die on the estate on her side of the tracks, to walk in her mum's footsteps? *It certainly looks like it,* she thought. *Alone, broke, and pregnant. I want to run away; I don't want to be me anymore, but how can I run away from this? How can I run away from my own choices, regardless of how irresponsible they were? I don't want to be my mum, but I can't ignore what's already inside my head and heart. I want this baby. I already love this tiny piece of life growing inside of me.*

'You really are a stupid bitch. What am I going to tell Sarah once you start running your mouth?' Ian snapped, enraged, as he pulled her out of her thoughts, leaning forward as he pointed his finger in her face.

'Sarah? What does Sarah have to do with this? Why do you have to tell her anything?' *Now I'm really confused. Why would he have to explain himself to his ex-girlfriend?*

'She's my FIANCÉE!' he shouted in her face. 'You know what? I'm done with this. I'm done with you, with Sarah, and with this ridiculous town,' he sneered as he pushed her roughly out of the way. He grabbed his jacket from the sofa and stormed out the door, deliberately slamming it on the way out.

Britney lost her balance and landed in a heap on the dirty floor. Pregnant. She had gotten pregnant by a piece of shit who not only used her and threw her away like yesterday's rubbish but who also had a fiancée he'd cheated on with her. *How stupid am I?* Britney sobbed. *The first man who gave me a little bit of attention, who made me feel like I was worth something, and I went and threw my body and heart at him like it was nothing. Now, look at me. Eighteen, knocked up, and sitting on the dirty kitchen floor of my mum's council flat with nowhere to go.*

Chapter One

TERRANCE CAFÉ

Present Day

'YOU DID IT, SARAH. You actually did it! Look at this place! It's incredible!' Brooke shrieked with delight. Brooke was a small, curvy woman with long, dark curly hair. But it was her big grey eyes and kind smile that managed to draw most people in. Brooke was Sarah's first employee as well as her best friend. They'd been through a lot together over the years, but their friendship had never faltered.

I can't believe I finally did it after all these years of hard work, scrimping and scraping every penny I had, Sarah pondered. Her blood, sweat, and tears had brought her to who she was today: the owner of Terrance Café, named after her grandfather who died more than a year ago. Sarah glanced around at her most outstanding achievement to date—one she'd accomplished all on her own.

The tang of freshly brewed coffee filled the air.

Keith caught Sarah's attention as he set up on the small stage in the corner of the newly painted area.

'Remember, Keith, a full set doesn't include flirting with every woman who walks by.' Sarah laughed.

Keith was a budding musician; he stood over six feet tall and had long brown hair that fell to his shoulders. He was incredibly gifted, but his lack of filter and propensity to say whatever came to mind always got him in trouble. On the other hand, his taste in women played a significant role in this as well.

'Yeah, yeah, got it. Oh, I've been meaning to ask you—if Jenny Moorfield comes in today, can you please make sure you seat her at the farthest table from me? I'm telling you, that bitch is crazy.' He snorted.

'Jenny Moorfield?' Sarah asked. 'What did you do now?'

'Nothing at all. I started seeing her a couple of weeks ago. At first, we hit it off. Then, after a couple of days, she became clingy as hell, texting me every hour of the day, and when I couldn't reply because I was busy at gigs or doing other stuff, she would walk around town looking for me and asking everyone in the local shops if they had seen me.' He snorted again as he leaned down to plug in his microphone. 'When I confronted her about it and told her to back the fuck off, she had some sort of mental breakdown and started accusing me of sleeping with every single woman I said hello to around town. That was it for me. I

ended it there and then, and ever since, she's been spreading all this bullshit about how I'm bad in bed to try to get back at me. That spiteful tramp can stay far away from me. She can kiss my arse.' He shook his head.

'I've told you to stop getting involved with these women. If it's not Jenny, it's Vicky from the beauty shop—'

Keith cut her off. 'Don't even mention Vicky! I still have nightmares about her.'

Sarah sighed as she shook her head. He never learned. Maybe one day. Keith had a taste for stunningly beautiful women who brought about more drama and were crazier than all the characters on any soap opera combined.

The commotion on the street disrupted Sarah's thoughts. It seemed to be getting busier; birds tweeting, loud chattering, banging, and laughing flooded her senses as people began to line up outside the front door. In comparison, the inside of the café appeared to be calm. Sarah took a few moments to take it all in, her gaze lingering on the round metallic tables scattered around the floor. Then, finally, she closed her eyes, counted to five, and was ready to go.

Brooke had already prepared herself behind the counter for the doors to open and the crowd to begin pouring in. 'I just double-checked with the kitchens. Pete and Mark are all ready to go,' she called to Sarah. Pete and Mark were the cooks Sarah had just hired a few days earlier. It took her a long time to find the right people, people she felt comfortable with looking after her customers. She hit it off with both of them right away. They were a married couple, both chefs who met at a conference ten years ago. Open, friendly, and professional. She knew she wanted them straight away.

'Let's open the doors, then,' Sarah said as she marched over to the entrance, slapped a bright, customer-friendly smile on her face, and unlocked the door, preparing herself for the opening day.

The sun was the first thing that hit Sarah, almost blinding her. The second was the massive crowd of people who had gathered outside to wait, some carrying bags, others laughing loudly with their friends or partners.

'Welcome to the opening of Terrance Café! Please come in and wait at the front counter. I will have your server, Brooke, come and seat you shortly,' she announced before she pulled the door wide open and placed a doorstop underneath it so one side of the two-door entrance would remain open.

Sarah walked over to the counter.

'Let's do this.' She smiled at Brooke.

Brooke headed towards the crowd and started seating them one by one. They complied and sat, taking the menus that Brooke handed to each of them with a smile. Most customers were in deep conversation with their companions, though they spared courteous nods for Brooke.

Sarah heard the soft strumming of a guitar begin and finally felt at peace with her life. Over the years, she had overcome so many obstacles, embarrassments, and agonising heartbreak. The first was with Jake, her first love, which she couldn't bear to think about even now. Second, when her then-fiancé Ian disappeared one evening into thin air; she'd found out a couple of weeks later that he left because he got another girl pregnant. Third was when her grandad died; he was her rock, her best friend, the only adult who had her back and best interests at heart growing up. *I hope he would have been proud of what I made happen today.* She smiled at the thought of him. *If he were still here, he would have sat at the table closest to the stage, shouting at Keith to play real music and none of this new-age crap, with a cup of steaming hot black coffee in his hand.*

'Sis, I love what you have done with the place. I've only got a couple of minutes, so I'll have a coffee to go,' a familiar voice shouted from the front door—her twin brother, Ryker.

Ryker was the resident hard man of this town, with his large muscular build, black hair, and blue-green eyes—a trait he shared with his siblings.

Ryker had respect from people from both sides of town, from the council estate to the big white houses on Eastern Street. But, honestly, most people tried to know as little as possible about what Ryker's so-called *business* entailed. They had good reasons for that. One, if he ever got caught, they wouldn't be a witness to any of his activities, and two, they preferred to stay on the good side of the law. Still, all Sarah saw was the twin brother who defended her against their family, looked out for her whenever she needed it, and used to sneak downstairs on Christmas Eve every year to help their older brother Dylan wrap her Christmas presents when they were kids—he still didn't know to this day that she knew. Meanwhile, their father, who was never home, would throw money at one of his young assistants, ask them to buy anything expensive, and shove the gifts into the corner of the house. Her mother would go on pretending for years that she did all the work, but Sarah knew the truth.

Sarah rushed over to her brother and hugged him. 'Thanks for coming. Can you believe I've finally done it? Grandad would be so proud.'

'He would. We're all proud of you. Speaking of family, where's Dylan?' Ryker scanned the room as he looked for their older brother.

'He couldn't make it. He sent me his best wishes, but he has to prepare for his first day tomorrow, and you know how he feels about large social engagements where people can ask questions.'

Dylan, their older brother, had recently moved back into town; he had left for university twelve years before and had only just returned. He was emotionally stunted. He'd be polite and engage in conversation, but it'd all be a ruse. Everything personal was off limits to him; he avoided crowds, awkward conversations, and places where people might question him about his past. But he hadn't always been that way. Dylan was the sweetest, kindest, and most openly loving man she had ever known. All of that changed five years ago, when his wife, Melissa, was killed in a tragic car accident. She was twenty-six at the time, the same age as Dylan. She had the rest of her life ahead of her. He shut himself down entirely after the accident, becoming colder and more distant over time. He left the city, down south, where he and Melissa had lived not long after. He'd been travelling ever since, most likely to find himself or, at the very least, to help him get over the agony of losing her, and now he was back. He had just secured a new job as a primary school teacher and was doing his best to keep a low profile.

'I guess, but he's starting work at Rovon Moore Primary. The mums there gossip more than the kids. How does he plan on avoiding nosy cows, then?' Ryker snorted.

He has a point. 'Your guess is as good as mine,' Sarah replied before turning towards Brooke, who was serving an older couple in the window seat. 'Brooke, can you grab Ryker a large coffee, black? To go, please!'

'Sure,' Brooke returned, smiling at Sarah and shooting a dirty look Ryker's way.

'I might make this my regular stop first thing in a morning—' Ryker began.

'I object!' Brooke snapped as she dashed past.

Ryker's eyes rolled towards the ceiling. 'This isn't a courtroom, short stuff.'

'Well, you would know all about them, wouldn't you?' Brooke scoffed.

He gave her a quick smirk before moving his gaze back to his sister. 'You should think about improving the customer service in here, sis,' he said as Brooke marched off in a huff.

'Do you always have to antagonise her?' Sarah groaned.

'What? I'm just standing here minding my own business.' He smirked before heading towards the counter, where his black coffee waited for him. 'I'll catch you later,' he said as he picked up his coffee and headed to the door. He passed Brooke—who was taking another customer's order—and smirked at her as he headed out.

Sarah rolled her eyes at him. You'd think she'd be used to Brooke and Ryker's childish behaviour around each other by now. But unfortunately, since they were kids, they had found ways to get under each other's skin and had yet to grow out of it.

'What a prick ... anyway, what time are the other girls getting here?' Brooke asked.

'Becky should be here in about ten minutes, and Megan isn't starting until two. So you take section two, and I'll cover section one until Becky gets here.'

Sarah raised her eyes to the large clock on the wall in the centre of the room. Just after ten a.m. Another ten hours to go. She grabbed a pen and a small notepad from the counter and proceeded to section one, near the front of the café.

Sarah approached a customer to take their order, but something caught her eye outside the window, across the street. She came to a halt. Her heartbeat quickened, and her palms became wet. Her feet felt glued to the floor, and a lump formed in her throat. She'd recognise that face from anywhere. Sarah hadn't seen him in ten years, but she spotted him all too easily. He was a boy the last time she saw him, and now he was a man. Her heart felt as if it was about to burst through her chest. She felt sick. She needed to back away, but she couldn't move. *One. Two. Three. Four.*

'Jake,' she whispered, her voice hoarse.

He didn't see her or even glance in her direction, just opened his car door and settled inside.

In an instant, a memory she had been trying to forget for years flooded back.

'My mum said I can't see you anymore,' Sarah whispered, her eyes filling with tears as she stared up at him.

'Fuck your mum ... listen,' Jake mumbled as he pulled her into his arms and rested his head on top of hers. *'I love you, and I will always look after you.'*

'But what if she ...'

Jake cut her off immediately. *'I will never leave you. Do you understand me?'*

A car horn from outside snapped Sarah out of her memory.

When did he come back into town? Why didn't anyone tell me? I could have prepared myself.

Chapter Two

ROVON MOORE

FOR BRITNEY ADAMSON, BEING on the playground of Rovon Moore Primary School was like being in the jungle. Everywhere she turned, beady eyes followed her, mother hens patiently waiting for her to take one step out of line so they could pounce. Dirty looks were directed towards her by women she had never even spoken to before, and hushed whispers faded into an awkward silence as she walked by. *They all need to give their heads a wobble. Stuck-up cows.* She snorted.

Britney looked down at her adorable son, Noah, who had her dirty blond hair and cheeky grin. His bright blue eyes mirrored those of his sperm-donor father, as Britney referred to Ian—that deadbeat had never done anything for Noah except disappear.

Britney hadn't seen or heard from him since he'd abandoned her on the filthy floor of that rundown council flat. She would have pursued him for child support, but she had no idea where he was. On the other hand, Britney didn't want him to have anything to do with her or her son.

It wasn't like he'd ever tried to reach out or even cared about knowing his son over the years anyway. The last Britney heard, the prick had married and moved to an unknown location.

After that dust-up with Ian, Britney picked herself up bit by bit off that cold, dirty floor and put a plan in motion for herself and her baby. She had been eighteen, alone, and scared, with no one to turn to. Her mum threw a fit and claimed Britney had ruined her life just like her own had been ruined after Britney was born. Luckily, Britney's NVQ Level 2 for hairdressing came in handy, and she got a job sweeping the floor at a local hairdresser's. From there, Britney worked her way up over the years, finally becoming an experienced hairdresser.

The most challenging phase in her life so far had to be the first year after Noah's birth. That day in the hospital had changed her. Britney was no longer the naïve little girl who had dreamed of someone rescuing her and taking her off the estate. Instead, she realised that she needed to save herself; no one else could do that for her.

Britney's son was the light of her life. He was the reason she got up every morning and started the daily grind. She'd promised herself that she would try to make a better life for him.

'Mummy, do I start the big class today?' her baby boy lisped as he grinned up at her. He was missing his two front teeth.

'Yes, sweetheart. You are starting year one. Are you excited to see your friends and your new teacher?'

'Freddie is in my class, and Asbelle will be there too!' He clapped happily. His best friends were Freddie Moorfield and Isabelle Beatly, although he couldn't pronounce Isabelle's name correctly yet. Freddie and Isabelle were both adorable kids, but their mothers were something else entirely. Jenny Moorfield and Liz Beatly always looked down their patronising, powdered noses at Britney, whispering and sniggering amongst themselves while trying to sneak glances at her. But of course, Britney Adamson, 'a dirty sket from the council estate,' knew precisely what they were thinking.

'Britney Adamson, is that you?' The loud shriek carried across the playground. *Oh, speak of the devil!* Britney turned to look at Liz Beatly as she marched towards her. Her long, wavy red hair framed a beautiful face, with long eyelashes fluttering over her chocolate brown eyes. Accompanying that hourglass figure was the adorable little Isabelle.

'Asbellllllle!' Noah hollered his excitement.

'Noaaaah!' came the screechy response from Isabelle.

'Hi, Liz, how are you this morning?' Britney asked politely.

'Oh, my morning's been hectic. Jonathon had to go to work early, so I got stuck with getting Isabelle ready. I've been so stressed out with the preparations for the new conservatory we are having built in, you know. So I'm going to yoga after leaving Isabelle here.' She sighed dramatically.

Liz Beatly was the type of woman who had never held a job a day in her life, and stayed at home as she fussed over pointless shit like tea parties and weekly brunch meetings when her child and husband were away. She could afford to do that, as her husband Jonathon Beatly owned a construction company in town.

How I wish my biggest problem was making adjustments to my own house. Britney snorted quietly. But then again, that would never happen, considering I rent a two-bedroom council flat and work as many hours as I can at the hairdresser's to keep myself and Noah afloat.

'Oh, that sounds rough.' Britney smiled tightly at her. 'But at least you have something to look forward to once you have your conservatory. So, the kids' new teacher, Mrs. Davies, seemed nice.'

'Mrs. Davies? Oh, no! Didn't the school make you aware? There were some last-minute changes this year due to a new arrival. You'll never guess who I heard was back in town and taking over the job—' Liz started, before a loud whistle sounded somewhere on the playground, blasting their eardrums.

'See you in class, Asbelle.' Noah grinned as he grabbed his mother's hand and waved to his little chum.

'That's our cue ... see you soon,' Britney said to Liz and her daughter. Already, older children were lining up in front of their teacher, ready to go inside.

They walked towards the school entrance and headed to their destination, Noah's new classroom for the year. The door was closed, so Britney knocked gently and waited.

The door quietly opened and... *Wow, he's gorgeous.* Britney thought as Mr. Take Your Breath Away walked out. He had dark brown hair and emotionless blue-green eyes. A deep frown settled on his face. He appeared to be familiar, but Britney couldn't place him. Five years ago, a man like this would have left her speechless, but that was before.

'Dylan—Dylan, do you remember me?' shouted Liz as she ran up behind Britney, her heels clicking on the floor.

'Oh, hi, Liz! How have you been?' he asked politely.

'Good. I see you finally met Britney,' Liz said. 'Well, let's hope this year doesn't get awkward, considering what she and Ian did to your poor sister,' she added with feigned concern.

Wait. What did she just say? His sister ... and Ian? Is this Sarah's brother? Britney groaned. *Trust my luck.*

'I'm sure we can all stay polite and professional, Mrs. Beatly, and I expect you to do the same,' Dylan said.

'Oh, of course,' Liz mumbled, a stricken look on her face. 'Forgive me for bringing up such a tragic episode.'

'Let's start again, then.' Dylan turned towards Britney. 'Lovely to meet you. I'm Dylan Colling, your son's new teacher. Sorry, the change was so last minute, and you must be Britney—I didn't catch your last name?'

Britney was baffled by how closed off this man appeared to be, even though he was saying all the right things. He seemed very polite, and he'd put Liz in her place, but his tone of voice and even his facial expression had not changed. It was a little unnerving.

'It's Adamson ... erm, Britney Adamson,' Britney murmured, embarrassed and unsure how to act in his company. Not only had she just found out he was Sarah Colling's brother—from Liz, of all people—but she also didn't seem to know how to communicate with him properly.

'I'm Noah.' Noah jumped in front of Britney and looked up at Dylan with a wide grin on his cute little face.

Dylan crouched to face Noah at eye level and put his hand out for Noah to shake.

'Lovely to meet you, young man. My name is Mr. Colling. I'm going to be your new teacher for the year,' he replied as Noah reached over and shook his hand.

'Mr. Coll, Mr. Coll, I'm Isabelle!' shrieked Isabelle as she pushed her mother out of the way and ran towards Dylan and Noah.

'Hello, Isabelle, it's lovely to meet you too. Come on in, then. Why don't you two go into the classroom and get settled? I will be with you in just a moment. I can see other parents coming through the door now with more of your new classmates,' he told the two children before he glanced back at Britney.

Liz quickly turned and fled down the corridor, without even saying goodbye to her daughter.

'Come say goodbye, sweetie,' Britney called softly.

Her little boy rushed up to her, grabbed her by the arm, and forced her to bend over so he could plant a wet kiss on her cheek.

'Bye, Mummy, love you.' He giggled before he scampered off into the classroom after Isabelle.

'It's nice to meet you, Mr. Colling. Hopefully, we will not let our family history get in the way, and we'll keep this relationship professional,' Britney told him politely.

'Of course, Britney. I know bits and pieces of what happened from my sister, but I know you didn't know and that what happened wasn't your fault. Let's wipe the slate clean, right? Your history with my sister doesn't have to be our history—or our present, for that matter.' He spoke firmly, with the same blank expression.

'Yes, I would like that very much, Mr. Colling. I will see you later, then, when I return to collect Noah.' She sighed in relief. *Hopefully this gets better, and I won't have to deal with any tense moments or awkward interactions in the future.*

'Call me Dylan, and see you soon,' he replied before turning and walking into the classroom.

Well, it's the first day of my son's new school year. I've already gotten a lot of dirty looks from other mums in the playground. Britney groaned as she stomped off. *Also, I had an unpleasant interaction with that bitch Liz Beatly, who went so far as to embarrass me in front of my son's new teacher, who also happens to be Sarah Colling's brother. Things can only get better from here.*

Chapter Three

THE BLUE BELL

'EXCUSE ME. EXCUSE ME, coming through!' Sarah yelled as she pushed her way through the crowded pub, grabbing Brooke's arm for good measure, so they didn't lose each other in the commotion.

Finally, she spotted a couple standing in a small booth and collecting their shopping bags from under the seats.

'QUICK!' she shouted as she ran towards the newly available table and threw herself and Brooke into the booth.

They'd been coming to The Blue Bell—the busiest pub in town—for years for the cheap drinks and for the down-to-earth owner, Dan. The only issue with the place was that it had seen a lot of drama and smackdowns over the years.

'Remind me again why I agreed to have drinks with you after ten on a Friday night?' Brooke groaned.

'Well, because you clearly love me, and we are celebrating. This is our first weekend since I opened the café.'

'True. I'm thinking cocktails?' Brooke smirked as she reached under the table for her black work bag.

'You know me so well, and put your purse away; drinks are on me.' Sarah chuckled, slapping Brooke's hand away from her bag and pulling her own purse out instead.

'There's Keith! He's standing at the bar with...' Brooke moved her head slightly as she looked over the shoulder of the couple seated at the table in front of them. 'Rosie Forrester?' Brooke returned her gaze to Sarah, her eyebrows raised.

'Rosie? Didn't she marry that butcher on Bakersmith Street?' Sarah's brows furrowed in surprise.

'The last I heard.' Brooke glanced back towards them and grumbled, 'I bet her husband doesn't know who she's with right now ... not that he won't find out, with how fast gossip spreads around here. Beware of Baynor Green, where everyone knows everything about everyone,' she mocked, holding up her hands dramatically.

Sarah erupted in laughter. *She had a point; the people around here think they belong on a soap opera.*

Sarah rose from her seat and pushed her way through the crowd to the bar.

'Sarah! SARAH!' A loud yelp startled her, and she turned to face a short, stout man who was practically gluing himself to her side.

'Do I know you?'

'Will you tell Ryker that I *swear* I have his money? It's just that—' He cut himself off as he ran a hand through his short, greasy dark hair. 'I'm having issues with the bank. You know how they are.' He laughed nervously. 'But I'll get it to him as soon as I can!'

'Do I look like his messenger? Tell him yourself,' Sarah said, rolling her eyes and pushing herself forward. She was sick and tired of strangers approaching her all over town, asking her to put a good word in for them to her brother.

'Get me two blue lagoons,' she said to the nearest server across the busy bar.

'Coming up!'

'How are you, Sarah Colling?' The loud yell came from behind her.

Sarah turned and came face to face with Crystal Shavis, who was beaming up at her with her bobbed grey hair, bright blue eyes hidden behind her glasses, and a massive handbag seemingly the size of her entire body.

Crystal Shavis was a tiny woman in her sixties who had been married five times and had spent her entire life meddling in other people's problems. She moved to town about eight years ago after her last husband died, and she had been giving Sarah's mother, Charisse, the town gossip queen, a run for her money ever since.

'I'm good, thank you. How are you?'

'Very well, thank you, dear. Are you here with Brooke?' she asked as she did a quick scan of the room.

'Two blue lagoons. Eight pounds, please,' the bartender interrupted as he placed both cocktails in front of them.

'Here, keep the change.' Sarah handed over a ten-pound note and glanced back at Crystal. 'Good to see you,' she said, grabbing her drinks and heading back to her table before Crystal could say anything else, or worse, invite herself to sit with them.

'Here.' Sarah handed one of the cocktails to Brooke. 'You got off easy. I ran into Crystal Shavis at the bar.' She groaned as she threw herself back into the booth.

Brooke laughed, but abruptly stopped when Cherry Walker approached their table.

Cherry Walker was one of Ryker's many flings. While she wanted more, he always shot her down and put her in her place about what he wanted out of their so-called *friendship*. Ryker had always been honest about his intentions with women from the start. Cherry was a leggy, naturally tanned brunette with an overconfident personality and the need to always be the centre of attention—*perhaps one of the reasons Ryker doesn't want a relationship with her,* Sarah thought.

'Hi Sarah,' Cherry said. 'Where's Ryker tonight?'

'Not sure,' Sarah replied, before she moved her eyes back to Brooke.

'Oh, well, if you see him, tell him I've been trying to call him for days now.' Cherry sulked.

'Will do, but he's been busy lately, so I haven't seen him much myself.'

'I don't know why he isn't calling me back. He knows better than this. I don't appreciate being treated like a mug.'

'Let me give you some advice if he's ignoring your calls. He most likely doesn't want to talk to you,' Brooke said, snapping her eyes towards Cherry.

'Who asked you?' Cherry snipped as she looked down her nose at Brooke and gave her a quick full-body glance in disgust.

'If you don't mind, we are just trying to have a drink in peace here,' Sarah interrupted.

'Fine!' Cherry snapped as she stormed off.

'What a smug cow,' Brooke remarked as she sipped her cocktail and looked around the room. She jerked her head back towards Sarah, a worried expression on her face.

'Are you okay?' Sarah asked.

'Whatever you do, don't look towards the bar!'

'What, why?'

'Let's just say a certain blond-haired, green-eyed, six-foot wanker just walked through the door,' she said, her voice trembling with concern. Straight away, Sarah knew who she was talking about. She told Brooke all about how she'd caught a glimpse of Jake across the street at the beginning of the week and how she hadn't seen him since; she had desperately hoped he was just here visiting family and had already left to go back down south. She couldn't deal with this right now. She was emotionally and physically exhausted after dedicating all of her time and energy to starting her new business. She had finally reached a point in her life where she felt she was in a good place. She didn't need the ache in her chest that hit when she'd first caught a glimpse of him through the café window days before, and how it now threatened to cut her in half as she ignored Brooke's warning and glanced across the room.

She spotted Jake as he strolled up to the bar. She glanced back towards Brooke, who offered her a soft, sympathetic smile.

'We can leave if you want,' Brooke said.

'No, this is my local. I won't let him run me out of it.' Sarah sighed as she picked up her drink and took large gulps, finishing it. 'I'll go and get the next round in!' She jumped up from her seat as Brooke reached over to stop her.

'Sarah, you don't have to do this!'

'I had to deal with this one day. Anyway, it's been ten years! I'm over it,' she snapped.

Brooke just offered her a doubtful expression before she let go of Sarah's arm and watched her make her way back over to the bar.

One, two, three, four... Sarah started to count. When her anxiety got the best of her, she would count to herself nonstop until she calmed down. It was her safety blanket. It started when she was a child and she would hear her parents screaming at each other from another room—on the rare occasions that her father was home. She would put her small hands over her ears and count for as long as she could until the fighting stopped. It was her way of coping in emotional situations, and it was the only thing that calmed her down over the years.

'Sarah!' Crystal yelled across the crowded bar, before she grabbed her arm and pulled her through the crowd.

Sarah noticed Jake's bright piercing green eyes, dark blond hair, and soft full lips. Her heart sank into her stomach. She wasn't ready. *One, two, three, four, five.* She began counting and felt sick. She couldn't do it.

She couldn't confront him about leaving. Not yet, not in front of all these people. Her heart was pounding, and her mind was racing with numbers as she continued to count. She couldn't do it; she couldn't do it...

'Thanks, darling.' He smirked flirtatiously at one of the female bartenders on shift, who blushed in response.

'Oh, I was just telling Jake about that new café you just opened.' Crystal said as she stepped in, drawing Jake's attention away from the pretty bartender and towards her.

As he came face to face with her, his flirtatious smirk vanished. 'Hello, Sarah,' he said.

'Hello, Jake,' Sarah mumbled, her gaze fixed on the beer-stained bar in front of her. *One, two, three, four...*

'Crystal has high praises for that new café of yours,' Jake said. 'I'm happy for you. I know it's something you have always wanted to do since you were a little girl.' His eyes softened slightly as he reached up to scratch the top of his eyebrow. A wave of nostalgia hit Sarah as she stopped counting and followed his movements. He always used to do this as a child when he was nervous. It helped her relax, knowing he was also feeling slightly on edge at seeing her again.

'Thank you, yes, it's a dream come true,' she answered as she planned her quick exit out of this awkward conversation.

She made an effort to avoid eye contact with him. She could deal with this, as long as he kept to small talk and didn't try to take the conversation any further.

'So, Jake, are you back here permanently or just visiting? Emma, my neighbour, thinks permanently, but I told her a chap like you would want to get back to the big city and not be stuck in this tiny town. I mean, you left it once already. How's your mother? Is she in here tonight?' Crystal probed nosily as she quickly glanced around the pub.

'She's not here tonight, no, and I'm not sure of my plans yet,' he answered, looking away as he gave the bartender, the same woman he was flirting with earlier, a brief smile. Sarah rolled her eyes at the display. He clearly hadn't grown out of his flirtatious behaviour, charming anyone he could.

'I'm sure you'll want to go back there soon! I mean, you've been living down there since you left for university. You took your pregnant mother with you at the time; I'm still shocked you let your poor mother and baby sister move back up here not long after to live on pennies while you were raking in the coins,' Crystal remarked.

Jake's face dropped and he quickly returned his gaze to the bar, but not before Sarah noticed the flash of pain in his eyes and the red tint that worked its way up from his neck to his cheeks.

'Crystal!' Sarah snapped through clenched teeth. 'How on earth do you know so much about Jake and his mother? Given that you moved to town after he left?'

'Oh, it's all over town. I heard from Emma, who heard from Caroline, who is friends with your mother.' Crystal turned her attention back to Jake as Sarah glanced down at the bar, seeking patience. 'So, Jake ...'

A loud commotion interrupted whatever Crystal was about to say.

'Rip the slag's hair out!'

'Isn't she married to someone else?'

'What the hell is going on?' Sarah yelled, pushing her way to the front of the crowd, where all the uproar was coming from.

Jenny Moorfield had a fistful of Rosie Forrester's hair.

'What are you doing? Get off me, you crazy bitch!' Rosie shrieked.

'Stay away from my man, you SLAG!' Jenny screamed in Rosie's face before she shoved her forward into a bar stool.

Keith threw himself in the middle of them before Jenny could grab hold of Rosie again.

'What the fuck are you doing?' he growled in Jenny's face.

'Is this why you left me? For this slag?' Jenny snapped as she tried to push past him to attack Rosie again.

'What I do is none of your business anymore!' he hissed.

'Break it up! Break it up! Jenny, this is the third time you have gone at someone in here this month. Leave before I ban you for life!' the owner, Dan, shouted as he ran out of one of the back rooms.

Jenny huffed. 'Wait till I see you again, BITCH!' she threatened Rosie before storming out of the pub with a vengeance.

Keith drew Rosie into the crook of his arm as he pushed past everyone, and rushed to get her out of the spotlight.

When everyone realised there was no more action, they immediately returned their attention to their groups.

'Keith! This is a married woman. Shame on you both!' Crystal shrieked as he rushed past with Rosie in tow. 'You just wait until I see your husband at the butcher's tomorrow.' She scowled at Rosie before storming off.

Sarah snorted loudly before pulling her lips tightly together, her face turning bright red in an attempt to suppress her laughter.

Keith turned to face her, puzzled when he saw her reaction.

'Do you need a shit or something?'

Sarah burst out laughing, head back, in full-blown hysterics. *I'm just done with today now,* she thought, howling. Rosie, Keith, and even Jake looked at her as if she had completely lost the plot. She couldn't stop herself from laughing so hard that tears were streaming down her cheeks.

'I think it's time for us to go now. I'll see you all later,' Brooke interrupted as she dragged Sarah off towards the exit.

'I think we finally broke her!' Keith said jokingly after them.

Funnily enough, Sarah thought as she let Brooke pull her out the door, *I was broken, but that was ten years ago, and I haven't been the same since.*

Chapter Four

The Call

SPAGHETTI HOOPS, SPAGHETTI HOOPS. There they are. Britney reached up to the top shelf on an aisle in her local supermarket and grabbed a couple of cans for Noah.

Spaghetti hoops, check.

She crossed the last item off her list and pushed her trolley towards the cashier.

'Britney Adamson.' A sharp tap on her shoulder brought her to a halt.

When she looked over, she saw a sickly, thin woman with a pasty complexion, dark circles under her eyes, and a haggard, scab-covered face staring back at her.

'Hi ... erm, do I know you?' Britney asked in confusion.

'It's me ... Ava O'Connor. We used to live in the same flats as kids.' She laughed loudly, drawing attention to herself.

Growing up, Ava O'Connor was one of the few people who was actually nice to Britney. She was a couple of years older, but she always made time to check in on Britney now and again. Ava lived a couple of floors below with her mum, and had a reputation among the lads on the estate, but Britney was never interested in gossip. With her long black wavy hair and light blue eyes, Ava was the type of girl whom lads would stop and stare at on the street. But as Britney looked into Ava's spaced-out eyes now, she realised the young girl she once knew was no longer there.

'Oh, yes, how have you been?' Britney winced at how formal she sounded.

'Good, yeah, listen, mate, you got a spare tenner so I can top up my electric?' she asked as she scratched her right arm.

'No, sorry, this is the last of it.' Britney grimaced as she returned to her shopping cart and unloaded it onto the counter.

'Oh right, well then, see ya later,' Ava grumbled as she walked away.

'Fifty-five pounds, please,' the cashier said, drawing Britney's attention.

'Here.' She handed her debit card over and began packing her shopping bags.

She hadn't seen Ava since Ava's mum died of an overdose when Ava was seventeen and Britney was fifteen. Ava vanished not long after that. She was well aware that Ava and her mum did not get along. Everyone in those flats used to hear them constantly yelling at each other. She had hoped Ava had found a way out and had settled down. Instead, it was clear from bumping into her that she had followed in her mum's footsteps. Britney only hoped she didn't meet the same fate.

Britney turned and walked out the front doors, carrying her large shopping bags, and smacked right into a hard body.

A familiar shriek startled her. 'Watch where you're fucking walking!' Britney glanced up into her mum's familiar eyes, a stricken expression on her face.

Britney had only seen her mum in passing over the years, and the last time they were this close was when she'd found out that Britney was pregnant. She'd completely lost her shit. Britney's recollection of that event flashed through her mind, remembering it like it was yesterday.

'PREGNANT? Didn't you learn from my mistakes? You know how hard this was for me. Why would you do this to yourself?' Melanie snarled at her daughter, disgusted.

'I didn't mean for this to happen. You should know that I'm keeping it,' Britney murmured.

'Keeping it? How the fuck are you going to look after a kid? You can't even look after yourself. Eighteen, and you're still here. You're lucky I even let you stay here after your child support stopped. You're not like me; you can't take care of yourself. You'll end up selling your arse to support that kid, or you'll dump the little shit on me. No, get rid of it. I'm not going to waste any more years of my life looking after some snot-nosed little shit,' she hissed.

'You won't have to look after it. I will. I'm only asking to stay here until I can sort a place out. I'll hopefully be gone by the time the baby comes,' Britney pleaded.

'NO! You either get rid, or you get the fuck out! I'm done cleaning up after you,' Melanie shrieked.

A car horn shook Britney out of her memory.

They were both staring at each other, not moving or breathing, barely making a sound.

'How is the little one?' her mum finally asked.

'He's good,' Britney replied bluntly, looking over her mum's shoulder to avoid her eyes.

She despised the fact that she was in this situation. Usually, if either of them saw the other from afar, they would turn and walk in the opposite direction, but when you accidentally bumped into someone, there was nowhere to hide.

'So, I heard you're doing all right at that hairdresser's.'

'Yes, I'm picking up a lot more shifts as business is good at the moment.'

'Well, I'm off meeting Joey,' her mum responded before waltzing past her daughter.

Britney was baffled for a moment as to who Joey was, but quickly realised he was most likely another of her mother's boyfriends. Not much seemed to have changed then. As she walked away, she felt her eyes sting as tears threatened to fill them. Sometimes Britney wished things were different. She wished she had the sober mother she had only ever seen glimpses of as a child. She took a deep breath and pushed the thought to the back of her mind. She had her son to think about now, and she didn't need anyone else in her life.

· · • • · • • · ·

'I WAS FUCKING BUZZING when Emma told me they knocked the price down for a decent haircut!' A loud shriek could be heard echoing throughout Bailey's Hairdressing Salon—or simply Bailey's, as the locals referred to it.

Bailey's was smack bang in the middle of town, between the council estate and the nicer part, so the clientele was diverse, just like at The Blue Bell.

'Speaking of Emma, you will never guess who she told me was back in town!' the bleached blonde in the salon's small waiting room said as she turned to a red-haired woman sitting in the seat next to her.

'Jake Cremell?' the redhead asked.

'No, Dylan Colling! But yeah, I heard about Jake Cremell showing back up in town too.'

'Well, my mum is friends with Jake's mum, and she told me he got involved in some big scandal at his fancy job down south, which is why he's come running back with his tail between his legs.'

'Really? Do you know what he did?' Blondie probed.

'No, but as soon as my mum finds out, I'll let you know.'

Britney rolled her eyes; another day in Bailey's equaled another gossip fest. She took a step towards them. Unfortunately, her twelve-o'clock client was one of these gossip queens.

'Amelia Renalds?' Britney asked.

'That's me.' The blonde jumped up from her seat.

'If you would come with me,' Britney said, walking over to one of the available chairs in the middle of the salon. Amelia, aka Blondie, followed her over and sat.

'I want a decent cut, still long, but cut my split ends off. I haven't had a good cut in a while, but when I saw this discount, I was straight on the blower.' Amelia smirked as she chewed her gum loudly. Britney's colleague sat Amelia's red-headed friend in the chair next to her.

'So, Amelia, you said Dylan Colling was back in town?' her friend said. 'I ain't seen him since he left for uni.'

'Oh, so I heard he met some bird at uni down south, settled down, got married, the whole shebang. She was killed in a car crash about five years ago. Anyway, he completely lost the plot after that, travelled to who knows where, and is now back,' Amelia explained animatedly. 'He's got a job at that primary school up the road.'

Britney's heart sank at her words. She'd never had anyone truly love her before. So it broke her heart to think about finding someone she'd want to spend the rest of her life with, marrying them, and planning a full future together, only to have it all ripped away in an instant, and then having nosy cows like Amelia and her friend talk about it as if you weren't a real person, and your tragedy was something to gossip about.

'How awful for him ... So, do you know if he's seeing anyone?' the redhead asked, raising her brows and grinning.

Is this bitch serious? Britney thought in anger. *She just heard about his loss, and the first thing she asks is if he's seeing anyone?*

'I'm not sure, to be honest, Cassie. Since he arrived back in town, he has kept to himself. I don't think anyone has seen him smile once. I just think he needs a good fuck. I went to his sister's café a couple of days ago and asked her if he was seeing anyone. The rude bitch just gave me a dirty look and walked off.' Amelia scoffed.

'Speaking of that family, what about Dylan's younger brother Ryker? Now, he is someone I wouldn't kick out of bed.' Cassie smirked.

'I don't think any of us would. Don't let Cherry Walker hear you say that, though. She will rip your head off.' Amelia snorted before looking up at Britney, slyly smirking. 'Oh yeah, you know his sister, Sarah, don't ya?'

Her friend quietly giggled at the remark.

I'm about to give this snotty bitch a taste of her own medicine. Britney's face scrunched up in anger. *To hell with her haircut; I'll cut the bitch's full head off*. Luckily, one of her colleagues, Lucy, interrupted with the salon phone in her hand.

'Britney, sorry to interrupt, but Noah's school is on the phone. They say it's urgent!' Lucy mumbled in concern as she passed the phone over to her.

'Hello?' Britney muttered into the receiver.

'Is this Miss Adamson?' came a hoarse voice on the other line.

'Yes, it is. Is something wrong?' Britney anxiously replied. *What if he's hurt? I don't know what I would do with myself if anything happened to him.*

'There's been an incident. Your son is fine, but we need you to come in. His teacher is requesting to see you urgently.'

'Okay, let me just get someone to cover the rest of my shift, and I'll be there as soon as I can.'

'Thank you. I will let his teacher know!' she replied before the line went dead.

Britney turned to face Lucy, who had been standing around waiting for the phone back.

'I need to go to school. It's Noah! Is there any way you could cover for me until Wendy comes in?' she pleaded.

'Of course! Let me know how it goes.'

'Thank you.' Britney smiled softly before she rushed off into the back room to grab her bag.

Chapter Five

FAMILY AND HEARTACHE

TEN YEARS AGO

SARAH LOVED SPENDING TIME with her grandfather Terrance when he came to visit; he was one of the only people who truly understood her. When she was little, she used to beg him to take her home with him so she could live with him and her grandmother, whom she adored. But her mother put a stop to that straight away. There was no way that she would let it get out around town that her only daughter left her to live with her grandparents. How would that look?

'Sarah! What on earth are you doing?' Her mother's loud bark rang through the room, startling her, and she jumped, dropping the packet of eggs she had taken from the fridge onto the floor. Sarah sighed at the mess and looked up at her mother.

'Will you leave her alone, Charisse? Look at the mess you caused now,' Terrance snapped through clenched teeth.

'The mess I caused? She's the one who dropped the eggs. Why is she even helping you cook anyway? You know she has to finish packing for university.' She glared.

'I wanted to help Grandad!' Sarah defended as she reached down to pick up the broken egg pieces and grabbed a mop from the kitchen corner.

'Clean this mess up! Oh, and your father won't be home to see you off. He will call you when he can, but I wouldn't hold my breath if I was you. He's too busy with his so-called *work* to be here for his family,' Charisse snapped before she threw a glare in Sarah's direction and stormed back out of the kitchen.

Her grandad knelt beside her and began to help clean up. He was staying with them for a few days due to some business he had in the area. He lived in a small village a couple of hours away with her grandma. He ran a catering business, which his daughter Charisse despised; he'd started from scratch and built his company from the ground up. Despite Charisse's family history, other family members frequently commented that she had forgotten her roots, and had a permanent stick shoved up her backside ever since she married Sarah's father.

Sarah's dream had always been to open a live-music café in town. However, her mother seemed to think it was a ridiculous delusion encouraged by her grandfather, and that she should instead focus all her energy on school, and the Accounting and Business Management course she was scheduled to begin in two days. What Charisse didn't know was what Sarah intended to do with the skills she gained from the course.

'Don't ever forget your dream. Do you hear me? You can do anything if you work hard for it.' He smiled as he leaned over and pulled her into a hug.

'I won't, Grandad, I promise.'

Sarah went to her bedroom to continue packing after she finished cleaning up. She was due to leave the following day, and the university she was going to was only an hour away, so she could still return whenever she pleased. Jake had been accepted to study at a university in London. No one was more surprised than he was, but Sarah knew that his years of hard work would eventually pay off. Jake excelled in all his GCSE and A-level exams, which was a shock to the system for many people. He applied to a few schools, but everyone knew the one in London was the one he wanted to attend. Sarah and Jake had planned to see each other every other weekend and talk at least once a day. They intended to return home and spend time together over the holidays. Everything had been carefully planned. Sure, they'd miss each other, but Sarah knew that if anyone could make it through, it'd be them.

Beep.

Sarah's phone vibrated with a text alert, so she picked it up and read the message.

Jake: I'm not sure this is going to work out. The distance will be too hard. So it's best if we just end it now. Don't try to contact me.

Sarah's heart dropped into her stomach. A wave of nausea overcame her. *One, two, three, four, five.* Her mind started racing. Maybe this was a joke? Not a funny or kind one, but that was the only explanation she could think of. Jake would never abandon her like that. She took a deep breath and tried to call his number, hoping she was right, that he was going to tell her it was all a bad joke, but as his phone rang and rang, a sharp agony struck her chest.

Rage. Humiliation. Pain.

She jumped to her feet. She'd go over to his, see what was going on, and hope like hell that it was a sick joke.

· · · · • · • · · ·

SARAH KNOCKED LOUDLY ON Jake's front door and stood back so he could see her through the peephole if he was inside. He'd have to face her. This joke had gone too far, and quite frankly, Sarah was pissed off. She looked up at the small run-down council house as she waited for someone to answer. Sarah had only been to Jake's house a couple of times; for reasons she never really understood, he always tried to avoid them going there as much as possible.

'Oi, where is she?' A hoarse voice from behind startled her. When Sarah turned to face it, she found a big beer gut, bald head, black teeth, and a face that hadn't been washed in weeks staring back at her. She was immediately repulsed, but she responded anyway.

'Who?'

'Cora!' he gruffed.

Cora was Jake's mother. Sarah had only met her a few times over the years, and each of those times, she had been completely out of it. On drugs or drink, she couldn't say, but it was never a pleasant experience.

'WHAT'S ALL THIS RACKET?' a tiny old lady yelled, peering out the neighbour's window.

'Sorry, I'm looking for Jake,' Sarah yelled back, her gaze shifting from the scruffy man in front of her to the elderly woman in the window.

'Well, you're too late. He left for uni not too long ago, took his pregnant mum with him. Now stop banging about. I'm trying to watch my soaps!' she huffed before slamming the window shut behind her.

Sarah began to count *one, two, three* before the pain slashed through her chest, and she collapsed to the ground when her legs could no longer support her. 'One, two, three, four, five,' she said aloud, rocking back and forth on the filthy floor of Jake's run-down front garden.

'What the fuck are you doing?' the repulsive man snapped.

Sarah's mind went blank, and all she could think about were the numbers in her head. Numbers didn't leave her. They weren't like her father, who would disappear for months or weeks at a time. They weren't like Jake, who just left without saying a word. They weren't like her mother, who would throw a parade over this, regardless of the pain that her daughter was in. 'Twenty, twenty-one ...' she continued as she rocked in despair. Numb. She had no idea that she was even crying until the drops hit her lips.

'I'm surrounded by crazy bitches. You tell that bitch Cora "Mike is looking for you" if you see her!' Mike snorted and stomped off, heaving his obese body in the opposite direction.

Sarah continued to rock and count while ignoring him.

· · · ● · ● · ● · · ·

'TRAMP!' YELLED A GROUP of local lads as they whizzed past Britney on their secondhand bikes.

She rolled her eyes, ignoring them, and continued up the estate, closing in on the filthy, run-down high-rise flats where she lived with her mum.

'Oi, sket! Don't ignore us. I heard your mum's slagging it around to anyone that wants it. Like mother, like daughter.' One of the little shits grinned crudely at her with a cigarette hanging out of his mouth. 'Zack Metford told us you wanked him off behind the black bins by the side of the flats,' he added, laughing.

'Zack talks shit! Everyone knows that!' she blurted in annoyance.

Zack Metford was a boy in Britney's year at school who lived in the same flats. He was also a lying prick. He was constantly going around the estate trying to big himself up, talking shit and making up lies to try to puff up his reputation with the other lads; at Britney's expense, this time, it seemed.

Britney flung open the red-stained door to the flats. There was a time when you entered a code to unlock it, but that had been broken for over a year now, and still no one had been out to fix it. She approached the elevator and noticed the out-of-service sign on the front, groaning. *At least our flat is only three floors up,* she thought. The floor was filthy, dark, and sticky, as if it hadn't been cleaned in years. Britney's old black school pumps clung to the floor as she walked, making a Velcro-like sound with each step. Her shoes had been falling apart for months. She constantly had to Sellotape the sole back on, which only gave the stuck-up bitches at school more ammunition against her.

Loud rap music filled Britney's ears as she approached the stairs and noticed one of her neighbours, Sean, with several large bags of weed, rolling a spliff and chatting with Ava. The lads on the estate always commented on how loose Ava was, but Britney ignored them. They talked so much shit that she couldn't tell what was real and what wasn't, and Ava was always so nice to her.

'Hey, Britney.' Ava smiled brightly.

'Hey.' Britney grinned in response.

'Want some?' Sean cast a glance her way as he pointed to a small bag.

'No, thanks,' Britney replied softly as she walked by quickly, trying to leave as much space between them as possible.

Sean was the local drug dealer, with foul body odour, scraggly beard, black teeth, and scrawny frame.

Britney dashed up the stairs to her floor and walked towards her door. She opened it after unlocking it with her key. As she walked into the run-down flat she called home, the smell of stale beer and ashy smoke hit her right in the face. Green wallpaper was peeling from the walls, and a mouldy blue carpet covered the small flat, which was littered with cigarette burns.

'Mum, are you home?' Britney yelled across the small flat to no response.

A loud banging echoed through the wall from the flat next door to her.

'I KNOW YOU FUCKED HER, YA BASTARD!' Britney heard her neighbour Mikaela scream from her flat. She sighed and rolled her eyes. Mikaela and Mike, her next-door neighbours, had a dramatic on-again, off again relationship. Mikaela worked part time at a nearby chip shop, and Mike just hung out in the flats all day, high. Britney saw him a lot as he wandered around the corridors looking for party favours. Mike didn't waste time after Mikaela brought home her wages, spending it on drugs and a twelve-pack from the local shop. *I guess he's shagging around on her now, too,* Britney thought. She didn't understand what Mikaela saw in him or why she continued to allow him back in the flat after throwing him out every other week.

Britney's stomach rumbled. She went into the kitchen and looked in the refrigerator; all she found was a mouldy half-eaten sandwich and a bottle of wine. She rolled her eyes and walked over to the cupboards, which, predictably, had nothing in them either.

Britney then remembered that she still had a packet of cheese and onion crisps in her school bag. Those would have to do. She walked into the cramped living room and tossed her schoolbag on the sofa, catching herself in the dirty, speck-stained mirror that had been chipped away at the corners. She looked at her shoulder-length hair, which had finally grown back. About a month ago, one of the main girls in her year at school who enjoyed making life hell for her, Jenny Moorfield, was seated behind Britney and snipped a large chunk of her dirty blond hair during art class. Britney's hair had been down to her waist before the incident, and it now only reached her shoulders. She went home in tears that day. Her hair was the only thing in her life that she felt she had control over, and it was ruined. Funnily enough, Jenny and Britney used to be friends in primary school, but then it all came out that Jenny's dad was shagging Britney's mum and was caught in the act by his wife, aka Jenny's mum. That was the end of that affair and also the end of the only friendship Britney had ever had. After that, Jenny completely turned against her and became one of the nastiest girls in school, constantly finding cruel ways to torture her ever since.

Since they couldn't afford to go to the hairdresser's and get it fixed, Britney's mum tried to make the best of what she could out of it with the kitchen scissors. Britney often thought that her mother wasn't all bad. When she was sober, which wasn't that often anymore. Once, a couple of years ago, she went a whole month without a drink, and it was the best month of Britney's life. They went for walks around town regularly and watched movies. She taught Britney how to put makeup on and even bought her some new dresses. Then a new man came into her mum's life, and she was back on the booze in no time. It was the drink and her constant desire to have a man in her life that was the issue. She was the type of woman who couldn't live without being involved with a man, which was why she was never alone—unlike her daughter.

The sound of the door creaking open grabbed Britney's attention.

'Britney, you home?' her mother's croaky voice shouted from the door.

'In here, Mum.'

Britney's hard-faced mother entered the room. She was once stunning with her long blond hair, chocolate brown eyes, and petite frame. Then the alcohol and hard partying took their toll, leaving her with ashy skin, dull hair usually shoved in a ponytail, crow's feet around her sunken sad eyes, and a very slim frame.

'I'm going out tonight. Don't know if I'll be home later. So I'll leave a couple of quid for you to get some chips for tea. I met the most charming man at the market today,' her mother began again cheerfully.

'That's great, Mum.' Britney plastered a fake smile on her face as she sat down on the sofa and reached for her homework from her school bag.

Britney's mum's last boyfriend, Tim, lasted at least three months, which she considered a long-term relationship. Tim had publicly dumped her in The Blue Bell for Zoey Starch, a sket who lived a few floors up. It was a massive brawl, and Melanie ended up with a huge black eye, while Zoey ended up with huge chunks of her dark hair missing. Melanie was barred from the pub for about a week before The Blue Bell owners lifted the ban. They must have realised that with the amount of time her mother spent there, she could keep the place afloat on her own. That incident occurred only three weeks ago. *I wonder what this new man would be called,* Britney thought.

'Mum, can I have an extra twenty? For some school shoes.'

'I'm not made of money, Britney. Those shoes you have on are fine,' she huffed as she plucked a pack of cigarettes out of her tiny black bag.

'No, the sole keeps coming off the bottom,' Britney complained as she pulled her school shoes off and shoved them in her mum's face. 'Look!'

'Then Sellotape it back on! Honestly, you kids nowadays have no appreciation for what you have! You are always demanding more.' She rolled her eyes. 'You have a bed, clothes on your back, and a roof over your head. Quit ya bitching. See, you're already killing my mood. That's it. I'm out of here.' She ferreted out a couple of coins from her bag and shoved them into Britney's bare hand. 'Here's a couple of quid for some chips. Don't wait up!' She hurried back out the door, leaving Britney in the company of the next-door neighbours, who were arguing once more.

One day, I will get out of this place, Britney thought, *and meet a cracking lad who won't care about my background, and we will get married and have children of our own. We won't be living here, though; no, we will be living on the nice side of town. Maybe he will be a doctor saving lives, and we could live on Eastern Street in those magnificent white houses. We will have a large garden, and our kids will get new shoes every week* ... She sighed. One could only dream.

Chapter Six

PROVOKED

PRESENT DAY

'I APPRECIATE YOU COMING in on such short notice.' Mrs. Atkin, the headteacher of Rovon Moore Primary School, said to Britney as she walked through the reception area's entrance door.

The receptionist turned to face them, looking up from her tiny desk in the corner and giving Britney a glance up and down before turning her nose up and returning her attention to her computer.

Britney rolled her eyes as she gave this stuck-up gesture little mind. *It's no skin off my back,* she thought before turning her full attention back to Mrs. Atkin.

'Yes, yes! Is Noah okay?' she asked.

'He's fine, as we told you over the phone, but he was in a fight with another boy in his class,' she explained as she removed her glasses and cleaned them with a small lens wipe that appeared out of nowhere.

Mrs. Atkin was tall and round, with large, circular glasses on her face. Her dark hair had hints of grey, and she wasn't a pleasant person to be around with her constant scowl.

'What? A fight? My Noah? There must have been a mistake,' Britney muttered in disbelief. *Noah is the happiest, sweetest kid on the planet. Getting involved in a fight doesn't sound like him at all.*

'Yes, please come to my office. His teacher is there now, waiting for us,' Mrs. Atkin stated sternly before stomping away. Britney followed her through the narrow corridors to her office, trying to come to terms with the fact that Noah had been involved in a fight. Mrs. Atkin slammed the door open, and Britney trailed behind, trying to keep her anxiety from boiling over.

The back of a man's head was the first thing she noticed as she entered the room. Dark, shiny hair. He turned towards them, and she was met with his bright blue-green eyes. Dylan Colling.

Mrs. Atkin glanced at Britney before moving her gaze to a small chair next to Dylan. Britney walked over to the empty chair and sat. Mrs. Atkin's agitated steps carried her to her oversized comfortable chair, positioned behind her desk.

'Your son has hit one of the other students in the face and started a fight in the middle of the classroom,' she said sternly, her nose in the air, her glasses slightly drooping on the bridge. 'As you know, we do not tolerate violence in this school.'

'There must have been a reason for him to act out like that. My son does not have a fighting bone in his body. He's a soft, sweet little boy,' Britney responded in a matter-of-fact tone, quite sure of herself. *Let her try to say differently,* she thought as she crossed her arms across her chest.

'As I was explaining to Mrs. Atkin …' Dylan paused for a moment to give the headteacher a stern look before returning his gaze to Britney.

'Noah was provoked by Freddie Moorfield,' he stated emphatically, his gaze unwavering.

Britney gazed at Dylan in disbelief. No one had ever stood up for her son before. A warmth she hadn't felt in a long time sparked in her chest, and a small smile threatened to break out across her face, but it faded quickly when her attention was returned to Mrs. Atkin.

'Words should not cause violence, Mr. Colling! As you well know!' Mrs. Atkin responded tightly.

'No, but when a student is provoked on a level like Noah was today, then the other child should be just as much to blame for the incident as Noah was.' He turned towards Britney. 'Freddie was baiting Noah and saying some cruel things to him.'

'Well, where is Freddie's mum right now? Why isn't she here?' Britney huffed at Mrs. Atkin.

'Mrs. Moorfield has been notified of the incident,' she responded firmly with a hard glint in her eye before continuing. 'However, we are here to discuss Noah's part in all of this, and his punishment. He will be suspended from school for two days. Hopefully, by then, *Miss*-Adamson, you could teach your son that fighting is not the way to handle conflict,' she finished.

'Two days? He's five years old. That's a bit much, don't you think?' Britney said.

'Again, we do not tolerate violence!'

'If Noah gets suspended for two days, then so should Freddie. As all students should be treated the same, isn't that right, Mrs. Atkin? That's part of your job, isn't it? The welfare of the students? You shouldn't be discriminating against any student while giving leeway to another student for the same offense, should you?' Dylan smirked at Mrs. Atkin, making no effort to conceal his condescending tone.

Britney's heartbeat quickened and her cheeks warmed; she couldn't stop the butterflies in her stomach. This man she'd met once was standing up for her and her son against his boss. He was standing up for her little boy.

Mrs. Atkin frowned. 'Yes, Mr. Colling, you are correct. Now I hope that *you* understand that personal attachments are not part of your contract,' she retorted before turning back to Britney.

'I expect better of Noah when he returns to school. I don't want to see anything like this again,' she said, twisting her face into an even more intense scowl than before.

'Noah is a good kid. You already know this, *Mrs. Atkin,* even if you don't want to admit it—' Britney began.

Mrs. Atkin cut her off. 'I'm not sure what you're trying to imply. I treat all my students with equal respect.'

'Look, Mrs. Atkin. Let's be real here. You have an issue with my son or me. Maybe even both, but if you don't want me to go to the school board about your unfair behaviour against my kid, I would cut the shit and treat him like you treat the rest. You get me?' Britney snapped as she pulled herself out of the tiny chair and stood at her full height, meeting Mrs. Atkin's eyes with an intense look of her own.

Gobsmacked, the headteacher replied, 'I treat all my students the same, and I apologize if it came across differently at all. That was not my intention.' She turned her eyes away from Britney and stared down at her desk.

'Don't worry. I will keep an eye on your son, Britney,' Dylan interjected.

'So, if you would please wait outside, Miss Adamson, your son will be brought to you.' She huffed as she stood up from her chair and motioned Britney out of the room. Britney started to follow her out, but before she did, she turned to Dylan, who was still sitting in one of the chairs. She leaned down slightly as she walked by. 'Thank you,' she whispered softly into his ear.

'You're welcome,' he responded politely before he quickly glanced away.

Britney left the room with a slight smile on her face. No one had ever defended Noah in such a way before, and she was happy Dylan had, especially since he had every reason to dislike her after what had happened with his sister.

She stood outside the room until Noah was finally brought to her. The woman escorting him happened to be the same woman from reception earlier; she appeared to be relieved to take a break from whatever she was previously working on. *Most likely Googling how to apply foundation without looking like a wotsit,* Britney thought, as she snorted at her bright orange face.

Noah approached Britney, his head down and a sad expression on his face. She felt a strong pull on her heart.

'Hi, sweetie! Come on!' she said, smiling down at him and reaching for his tiny hand.

'I'm sorry, Mummy,' he whimpered as he placed his small hand into hers.

They quietly exited the front reception area and began the fifteen-minute walk back to their apartment building. She looked down at Noah once they were a few streets away from the school.

'So, what happened today?' she asked.

'Freddie said I don't have a daddy because he was embarrassed to have a scruffy son like me with old shoes and soggy cheese butties,' he said softly and sadly, lisping heavily.

'Why would Freddie say something like that? I thought you were friends.'

'Freddie is a meanie now. He told Asbelle he only sees his daddy every other weekend now. His daddy has a new baby,' he responded, struggling to get all his words out without lisping.

Britney had learnt about Freddie's father abandoning him and his mother, Jenny Moorfield, about a year ago, but he remained in Freddie's life and always made time for him every weekend. According to Liz Beatly, at least. Liz never passed up an opportunity to ridicule anyone or anything, including her alleged best friend, Jenny. Freddie's father recently had a child with Tracy, his twenty-two-year-old girlfriend—the same woman he'd left Freddie's mother for. Perhaps this has had a negative impact on Freddie's behaviour. Jenny had been scouring the town for any man she could get her hands on ever since.

'Listen to me.' Britney stopped and crouched in front of him. 'You have me. You will always have me, no matter what, okay? Don't listen to Freddie. He has things going on in his life that are making him very angry lately, but that has nothing to do with you.' She reached over and gave him a reassuring kiss on his forehead before she stood and continued, 'But you should never hit someone again like you did today, okay? It's not okay. I understand that he hurt your feelings, but please don't do it again.'

'I know I'm sorry, Mummy. Never again. Promise,' he lisped before wrapping his arms around her and hugging her. She gently squeezed him back before they continued their walk home.

Once they got back to their flat. Britney started cooking Noah some food and got her phone out to call her boss, Wendy, at work.

'Ello,' Wendy's croaky voice answered.

'Hi, Wendy, it's Britney. I was wondering if I could ask you a big favour.'

'What is it?' she mumbled, disinterested.

'There have been some problems at school and Noah needs to stay home, and as you know, I won't be able to afford a babysitter. Is there any way you can give me the next couple of days off?' she pleaded.

'Sorry, hun, I can't. We are jam packed this week, and if you don't come in, I can't pay you for any leave. Due to it being such last-minute notice, and we need you.' Britney heard gum-smacking on the other end of the line. Wendy Hedred was a forty-two-year-old bleached blonde obsessed with Botox and acting like she was still in her twenties. Britney would say it was a midlife crisis, but she'd been this way since they met four years ago, when she took over the salon.

'Look, Wendy, can you please help me out? I'm in a bit of a hard place here.' Britney sighed before she continued, 'I'm not leaving Noah on his own, but I really can't afford the time off.'

'Look, why don't you bring Noah in?' Wendy relented. 'I'm sure he can sit in one of the back rooms with some colouring books and toys for a couple of hours.'

'Thank you so much.' Britney sighed in relief.

'You're welcome. Catch you later,' Wendy said before the line went dead. At least she wouldn't have to miss a couple of days' work.

Chapter Seven

THE UNANNOUNCED

'I DON'T CARE ABOUT the reason. Stop parking at the front of the café entrance like you own the street,' Brooke snapped from the front door.

What the hell is going on now? Sarah thought as she rolled her eyes and walked towards them.

Ryker's face darkened with rage before he cut Brooke off. 'Listen … I came in to grab a drink. It's not like I'm leaving it parked there. It would have taken two minutes, but with you standing here bitching and wasting my fucking time, that two minutes has now turned into five. Now move your fat fucking arse and let me get my coffee.'

Brooke frowned, a distraught expression on her face. Her anguish was palpable as she stood there at a loss for words. Ryker and Brooke had always fought, but he'd never shown Brooke this side of himself. Of course, it had been seen a lot over the years, but it had never been directed at her. Instead, Brooke and Ryker's disdain had always been expressed through childish banter. Nothing serious.

'What's going on?' Sarah interrupted quickly.

'He parked at the front entrance—' Brooke muttered before cutting herself off. 'I'll leave you to deal with this. I have some customers I have to attend to,' she said quickly before hurrying away.

'What's that about? I've never seen you snap at her like that before,' Sarah said, moving her gaze to Ryker.

'I've had a rough morning, and all I wanted was a quick cup of coffee, and someone still seems to be bitching at me. I can't catch a fucking break,' he snapped in frustration as he ran his fingers through his dark hair. 'Get me a coffee, black, to go. I've got some shit I have to take care of.'

I have no idea what's happened, Sarah thought, *but it must be bad for him to lose his cool in public.* Ryker was a man who kept his emotions under wraps most of the time. The majority of the town saw him with his cool, collected expression on a regular basis. Sarah had only seen him lose his cool twice due to different circumstances; one was related to their mother, and the other was when Ian had skipped town—Ryker wanted to go after him and sort him out, but Sarah begged him not to as she just wanted to move on with her life and didn't think Ian was worth it.

'Chloe, will you grab Ryker a black coffee to go?' Sarah shouted over to the counter.

'Thanks, sis,' he muttered as he stuffed his hands into his jacket pockets.

'Well, well! I see someone finally got their dream place.' A familiar voice pulled her attention away from Ryker. She turned to face the café's entrance and saw their older brother, Dylan, approaching them.

Sarah should have gotten used to his one robotic expression by now. Her heart ached and yearned for her smiling, sweet older brother, but he was no longer with her. He'd died that day in the accident, along with his wife.

'Dylan! I'm so happy you have finally graced us with your presence.'

'Yeah, yeah.' He rolled his eyes before continuing. 'Seriously, Sarah, this place is fantastic!' He looked around the room.

'I know! I love it! I can't believe you have been back in town for two weeks, and this is only the second time I've seen you. You're slacking!' She smirked and lightly punched his arm.

'You know how hectic it's been. I told you plenty of times over the phone. I was moving into my new place across town. I started my new job at the school Monday just gone,' he said. 'How about we make time to at least see each other once a week, maybe more if we can. Deal?'

'Deal! How's your new job going?'

'All right. I've already had to deal with a fight today.' He sighed.

'Yeah, who won? Was it a good one?' Ryker interrupted, smirking.

'Well, strangely enough, it was between Jenny's son, Freddie Moorfield, and Noah Adamson,' he mumbled awkwardly.

'Wait, as in—?' Sarah began.

Dylan replied, 'Yes, Britney Adamson's son.'

'You're her kid's teacher?' Ryker asked, his brow furrowed.

'He's a good kid. Seems to be constantly looked down upon for the sins of his father,' Dylan grumbled.

'And his mother,' Ryker snorted.

'It wasn't her fault. She didn't know, as you well know,' Sarah jumped in. 'We never really spoke after it happened—or before, for that matter—but she made an effort to write me that letter not long after Ian left, explaining everything that happened,' she defended softly.

Sarah and Britney were not what anyone would call friends or even acquaintances, as they had never even interacted in person. They'd passed each other on the street or in the supermarket over the years, but they'd never said anything. Not long after Ian left, Britney posted a letter through Sarah's front door, explaining her entire relationship with him. Sarah didn't respond at the time because she didn't know how, but she never forgot it.

'Yeah, give her a break. From what I've witnessed,' Dylan said in annoyance, 'the teachers and the parents at the school are real arseholes to her.'

'Of course, Super Dylan to the rescue,' Ryker remarked.

What the hell has gotten into him today? First Brooke, now Dylan. At least Keith had perfect timing for the first time in his life as he walked into the café to get his usual cup of coffee. Sarah had scheduled for Keith to spend his evenings playing live at the café until it closed at 10 p.m., and then he would spend his nights playing at gigs outside of town. As a result, he spent the majority of his days in bed. Then, finally, he would arrive for his regular coffee at four-thirty in the afternoon.

Sarah grabbed his arm and pulled him to a halt.

'Dylan, have you met Keith? This is the one who got involved with crazy Jenny.' She laughed as she shifted the conversation away from Ryker's bad mood.

'She needs to let it go. Honestly, I think women in this town are hiding from me now since they heard about what went down in The Blue Bell the other night.' Keith rolled his eyes.

'Nice to meet you, man. I teach Jenny's kid at school.' Dylan gave a slight nod.

'So you're the mysterious big brother. I thought they made you up.'
He smirked. 'Nice to meet you. Freddie is a good kid. Shame he has a
complete nutcase for a mother, though.' Keith sighed.

'Here's your coffee, Ryker,' Chloe interrupted as she handed over his
coffee to go.

'Thanks. Here.' He dropped two pounds into her palm and turned
back towards his siblings. 'I'm off! People to see and all that,' he grumbled
as he stomped out the door.

'What's crawled up his arse?' Dylan asked, puzzled.

'Who knows? Anyway, I'm glad you're settling in well. How's the new
apartment coming along?' Sarah asked to strike up new conversation.

· · ● ● · ● ● · · ·

'IT'S TIME FOR ME to clock out. Do you want me to stay and help
you clean up?' Brooke mumbled.

She'd been acting this way since her argument with Ryker earlier. Her
mood had been off all night.

'No, this is fine. You go ahead.' Sarah gestured her to the back room
as she approached the counter to begin cleaning the coffee machine. She
couldn't wait to get back home and sleep. It had been a hectic night.

Brooke appeared from the back room a few minutes later.

'I'll see you tomorrow.' Brooke smiled briefly as she walked out the
front door.

Sarah continued to clean the café, losing track of time, until she was
interrupted by a soft clearing of the throat. She looked towards the sound
and saw the same green eyes that she used to get lost in.

'Are you a prude or just a stuck-up bitch?' Bill Newman snapped as he attempted to pull her blazer off.

'Get off me now, Billy, before I tell the headteacher.' Sarah panicked as she leaned away from him.

Billy Newman was always trying to find ways to get her alone. She couldn't understand why, ever since she'd turned him down when he asked her to be his girlfriend two weeks ago, he couldn't just accept that no meant no and leave her alone. She hadn't told Jake about it; she didn't want to come across as the weak girl who couldn't defend herself. She was strong. So what if she started to count in her head when she'd spotted Billy in the corridor? She was Sarah Colling, and she would fight her own battles. She had come up against worse than Billy before. Like her own mother, for one.

'I bet you would as well. You're such a snitch—' he started before a slight tap cut him off on his shoulder. He turned and met Jake's fist to his face.

Billy left her alone after that.

'We close in five minutes, so you'll have to order to go, and I've just turned off the coffee machine,' Sarah said as she pulled herself out of the memory. She hoped she came across as carefree, despite the fact that her entire body was on high alert.

'Yeah, sorry. Can I have tea then, please?' Jake asked as he looked down at her, and for a brief moment, she thought her heart had stopped. *One, two, three, four.*

For the next couple of minutes, as Sarah prepared his cup of tea to go, she continued to count, and the silence that descended across the café was so awkward, she could have heard a pin drop.

She felt a protective tug on her heart and knew she needed to be strong. She couldn't wimp out again, even if she couldn't confront him head on. She could still make things difficult for him.

'Here. Three pounds,' she said as she set his drink on the counter.

'I thought it was one fifty. That's what your menu says,' he responded, looking up at the oversized menu on the wall to the side of the counter.

'Yes, well, I'm about to close up, so I added a little extra for my efforts.' She smirked as she extended her hand.

He sighed and reached into his pocket, slipping the pounds into her palm.

'You were much more polite when I last saw you, in The Blue Bell,' he remarked.

'Because you caught me off guard after a drink. I'm feeling very much like myself right now.' Sarah turned her back on him and continued to clean up, hoping he'd get the hint and leave.

'It's a shame. I was hoping we could put the past behind us and be friends,' he said wistfully.

Sarah snapped her head back to him. *He must be fucking kidding me, right?*

'Would you please leave?' Her voice trailed off into a bitter whisper.

'If that's what you want.'

'It is. Look, I don't want things to be awkward between us, so I'll try to tone it down, but I also don't think we could ever be friends.' She sighed. 'I'd appreciate it if you could just stay out of my way.' Defeated, she hoped he'd get the hint and leave her alone. She wasn't sure how long she could keep the bravado up before collapsing. She was never going to let him see her vulnerable again.

'I'm not sure if I can do that—' he mumbled as he averted his gaze.

'Well, you'll have to,' she snapped, cutting him off.

'I'll see you later.' He gave a soft smile as he walked out the front door, not looking back.

Sarah tracked his movements until he was out of sight. She couldn't understand why he wanted to be friends, or friendly, or whatever. He was the one who'd tossed her aside with ease. He didn't even tell her when he was leaving. He just walked away. For fuck's sake, he'd broken up with her over text and then just waltzed back into town over ten years later, as if it was a minor misunderstanding, as if it hadn't ripped her open. And now he wanted to be friends. He had another thing coming. The cheek of it amazed her.

Fuming. Raging. She could feel her blood boiling beneath her skin. She took her phone from her back pocket and called Brooke.

'You okay? I only left about ten minutes ago,' Brooke answered.

'Guess who just walked in a couple of minutes after you left, asking if we could be friends?'

'Jake?' Brooke groaned. 'I hope you told him where he can go.'

'I told him it wasn't happening and to leave me alone.'

'Do you need me to come back? Are you okay?'

'I'm fine. What was all that about between you and Ryker before?' Sarah asked. She'd been wondering about it since it happened earlier, but she'd wanted to give Brooke time to process whatever it was first.

'I don't know. I've never seen him react to me like that before,' Brooke sighed.

'I'll talk to him.'

'No, leave it. We're probably just overthinking it. Maybe he just had a bad day.'

'Okay. I'm about to lock up, so I'll talk to you later.' Sarah hung up the phone and stuffed it back into her back pocket.

She wondered if Jake and Ryker had run into each other yet. They were friends. Ryker didn't seem to react much when Jake left without a word, just like he didn't react much to anything. That was why today was such a shock.

Sarah's phone vibrated in her back pocket.

Ryker: Tell Brooke I'm sorry.

Sarah huffed and rolled her eyes. She couldn't figure out why he couldn't just tell her himself, but that was Ryker for you. She forwarded the text to Brooke, who responded immediately.

Brooke: Tell him it's all right.

What am I, a pigeon? She forwarded that message and then wrote a new one for both of them.

Sarah: It's not hard to text each other if you have something to say, instead of using me as a messenger. This is the last time I'm doing this. Next time, message each other. I know you both have the other's number as I gave it to you. Use it.

That will show them. Sarah chuckled.

Chapter Eight

DALECREME PARK

'THEN GUESS WHAT ASBELLE did, Mummy?' Noah smiled, his mouth full of chewed-up burger.

'What did she do? And eat with your mouth closed. I've told you this plenty of times,' Britney responded softly as she continued to clean the living room while Noah sat on the sofa with a half-eaten burger on his lap.

'Well, she kicked Freddie in the legs.' He burst out laughing.

'That's not very nice of her,' she said as she dusted the sides of the small TV.

'Freddie deserved it, Mummy. He was a big poo head.' He continued to laugh as he reached for the last of his burger.

It had been a week since Noah was suspended from school for two days. Since being back, he hadn't caused any issues, but that didn't mean that some of the other kids hadn't been acting up.

'Come on, get dressed, and we'll go to the park,' she said as he finished his burger and handed her his plate.

'Yayyyy!' He jumped to his feet and dashed into his small bedroom to put on his coat and shoes.

Britney and Noah took the twenty-minute walk down to Dalecreme Park every Sunday morning. It was in a more upscale neighbourhood, and the closest park to them not overrun with groups of teenagers high on drugs and/or selling them openly.

Noah came running out of his bedroom a few minutes later, dressed in his oversized blue bubble coat and ready to go.

'Ready! Let's go, Mummy, let's go!' he yelled as he dashed to the door.

Britney laughed and reached for her coat before sprinting over to tickle Noah as they opened the front door to leave. His tiny giggle made her heart melt.

They walked out the flat door, locking it behind them, and began their walk through the halls towards the elevator.

'Hi, Mr. Bealt. Hi, Miss Roasha.' Noah smiled and waved to two of their neighbours as they walked down the hall to the elevator on their way to the ground floor.

On their way to the park, Noah continued to tell his mother the latest of what was going on with his school friends.

Then, 'Mummy,' he said quietly, breaking off from his previous stories.

'Yes?' she replied, looking down at him with concern due to Noah's quick change of tone.

'Who is that old lady staring at me over there?' he questioned, looking down at the ground.

Britney shifted her gaze to the corner store on the other side of the street, her heart pounding loudly in her chest. A small figure stood outside, frozen, staring at Noah, her face drained of colour as she realised she had been caught. Britney instantly recognized the person as Jill Hennering, Ian's mother and Noah's grandmother. She had seen Jill around town over the years, but Jill had always gone out of her way to avoid Britney, choosing to walk in the opposite direction if they ever crossed paths. However, this was the first time Noah had noticed Jill staring and wondered who it was. Jill turned and ran into the shop as soon as she realised Noah was staring back at her.

'No one! So, tell me about what you did for arts and crafts,' Britney said, changing the subject.

Noah stopped in his tracks once they were about five minutes away from the park.

'Look, Mummy! It's Mr. Coll!' Noah shrieked in excitement as he pointed across the street.

Britney gazed in the direction that Noah pointed in and saw none other than Dylan Colling walking down the street, dressed casually in blue jeans and a black top, holding a small white shopping bag.

'Mr. Coll! Mr. Coll!' Noah yelled.

Dylan cast a glance their way. He gave them a slight nod before slowly walking across the street towards them.

He knelt politely beside Noah and extended his hand to shake when he got to them. 'Hello, Noah. How are you doing today?'

Britney let out a muffled snort at the display. She was baffled by the constant handshake routine.

'Good, Mr. Coll. We are going to the park. You can come too!' he yelped in excitement.

'Only if it's okay with your mum,' he said as he looked up at Britney and straightened to his full height, his gaze never leaving hers.

'It's fine with me. But I'm sure you're busy,' she said, looking down at his shopping bag.

He followed her gaze before lifting his bag slightly. 'Oh, this? I was just on my way back home from the shop. I only live a couple of streets away from here,' he replied.

'Then you can come, right, Mr. Coll?' Noah jumped up and down, grinning.

'Sure.'

Britney was bewildered as to how someone who appeared to be antisocial—based on what she had seen and heard—would agree to go to the park with them. Especially given that he was Noah's teacher. She shrugged and brushed it off for the time being. She hadn't forgotten about him defending Noah, after all.

They made small talk as they walked the next couple of streets over to the park. Noah mostly grilled Dylan on who his favourite superhero was. Noah insisted on going on the slide when they arrived at the park, while Britney and Dylan sat on one of the park benches.

'Thank you for keeping an eye out for him. It means a lot to me. He really looks up to you,' Britney said softly, turning her head and looking at him.

'He's a good kid. You're lucky to have him,' he replied.

'I count my lucky stars for him every day. I wish he was conceived under better circumstances and had a father who wanted and appreciated him.'

'That man is a fool. He doesn't know how lucky he is to have this. My late wife, Melissa, and I were planning to start a family shortly before her death five years ago. I still wonder what that would have been like, to be a father.' A shadow of grief echoed across his face.

'I'm so sorry for your loss. I'm sure you would have made an excellent father. I've seen how you are with the children at the school; you're amazing with them. You're such a good influence on Noah. He's constantly coming home with stories about what he learned from "Mr. Coll" today,' she said, despite the fact that 'Mr. Coll' was closed off and antisocial with the adults. She saw the respect and admiration the children at that school, including her son, had for him. She smiled at the thought.

His piercing blue-green eyes were dazed as he looked down at her. His lips twitched up slightly as he gave her a barely noticeable smile. She responded with a beaming grin. It was the first time she had ever seen him smile, even if it was only a small one, and she would take whatever she could get. She thought back to the conversation she'd overheard at the hairdresser's, about how no one had seen him smile since he'd returned to town, and wondered if that included this slight turn of the mouth.

'From what I've seen,' he said, 'you seem like an excellent mother, with everything life has thrown at you, and you still manage to stand tall for your son.'

'I could say the same to you—' She cut herself off softly as she got lost in his piercing gaze before she snapped herself out of it. 'I mean, with everything you have been through ... that you still manage to stand tall. Not that you have a son or anything.' She cringed, her words jumbled.

He let out a long sigh before answering. 'Yes, I understood what you meant.'

'So what brought you back to town?' Britney asked with interest. 'I don't know much about you, other than what I've overheard some of the women talk about around town.'

'Following the death of my wife. I just wanted to get away, you know.' He paused, looking away from her to the other side of the park, trying to hide his reaction. But the pain and longing on his face was palpable. 'I went travelling around Europe—Spain, Italy, Greece, Germany, France. I wouldn't stay in one place for too long,' he said, closing his eyes and shaking his head. 'I'd take odd jobs here and there, mostly teaching English in schools or odd bar jobs.' He turned and caught her gaze once more.

'Oh, wow! I've never left Baynor Green! I would be buzzing my tits off if I could ever get to visit even one of those places, never mind them all.'

Britney had seen pictures of other countries, but the closest thing she'd had to a holiday was a trip to Blackpool, and even then, she had to get the train on her own. She was able to afford it after selling enough of her mum's cigarettes at school.

'Buzzing your what off?' he asked with a dumbfounded expression on his face.

Britney burst out laughing as she wondered how on earth this man had lived in this town his whole childhood and had never heard that saying. She used to hear it every day, especially after someone in her local shop had won a fiver on a scratch card.

'It just means I'd be proper happy if I got to do it.' She chuckled as she wiped the small tears of laughter from her eyes.

'Mummy! MUMMY!' A loud giggle interrupted their conversation.

Britney turned towards Noah, who was running towards them.

'Can we have Macdon after?' he pleaded.

'No, not today. You had a burger at home earlier.'

'Oh, okay.' He pouted, a grim expression on his face.

'How about we get some McDonald's next week?' she said, trying to compromise with him.

'Yayyyyy!' His eyes and face lit up as he dashed towards the climbing frame.

· · · · ●· ● · · · ·

BRITNEY SMILED SOFTLY AS she turned her gaze to the park's swing set. Her heartstrings pulled as she heard a small giggle across the playground from her little boy, who swung back and forth on the swings with a bright smile on his face. Dylan was behind him, pushing him, and that slight smile he had shown earlier had returned at Noah's reaction. She stood up from the blue bench stationed in the middle of the park and walked over towards them.

'It's time to go.' She smiled.

'Ten more minutes, Mummy, please?' Noah begged, his gap-toothed smile wide.

'No, you said that twenty minutes ago. Come on, get a move on,' she said, reaching out to grab his hand.

'Mr. Coll, you want to come round our house for tea? Mummy is making sspagseti?' He grinned widely up at Dylan as he tried to pronounce spaghetti.

'I'm sorry, Noah, but I have dinner plans for tonight,' he replied.

'Oh ... that's okay, Mr. Coll.' Noah forced a smile on his face as he tried to hide his disappointment.

'How about another time?' he asked Noah quickly before he glanced at Britney. 'If that's okay with your mother.'

'YES! I mean ... yes, that would be great. Would it be possible to have your number? You know, just in case I ever need to contact you for any reason, like Noah and that, or not ... if it's not appropriate?' Britney mumbled, cringing hard at how that entire sentence came out. She wanted to shove a paper bag over her head and flee in embarrassment.

'Sure. I could use a new friend around here.' He reached for his phone in his jacket pocket and handed it to her. 'Just put your number in, and I'll call you so you have mine.'

Britney quickly typed her phone number into his phone and handed it back to him. He one-belled her phone straight away so that she had his number in return.

'Anyway, we have to get going. It was nice to see you,' she said confidently, attempting to reclaim some of her dignity.

'All right. I'll see you in class.' He looked down at Noah and then up at Britney, saying, 'Hopefully, I'll hear from you soon.' Then he turned and walked away.

'Can I watch cartoons when we get home, Mummy?' Noah asked as he pulled on her hand and drew her attention away from a retreating Dylan.

'Of course, sweetie! Come on, let's get going,' she replied as they walked out of the park hand in hand.

After the walk home, during which they played a game of I Spy, Britney thought a lot about Sarah. Maybe it was because she was Dylan's sister. Perhaps she just wanted to step up and clear the air once and for all, but she knew she was finally ready to explain herself.

Britney felt a vibration in her jacket pocket as they approached their flat's front door. She took out her phone and noticed an incoming text.

Dylan: It was nice to make a new friend today. Hopefully, we can do something like today again soon ▢

She grinned at the word *friend*, and her heart leaped. No one had called her their friend since she was a little girl.

Britney: Does that mean I can officially pick a nickname out for you for my contact list without you getting offended? Being my new friend and all. :D

She smiled at her reply and noticed that her message was read immediately before there was another incoming text.

Dylan: Only if I can pick yours, but "It's Britney, bitch" was already taken over twenty years ago :D so I'll have to have a good think on this one.

Dylan: And before you say anything, yes, I'm already cringing at that last text I sent you.

····•··•····

BRITNEY WAS TENSE AS hell. All she was doing was dropping her son off at school, just like any other Monday morning. The only difference was that she had spent hours the night before texting back and forth with his teacher, quite a lot given that she'd only received his phone number yesterday. She was glad she had unlimited texts on her phone as part of her contract, or her phone bill would have skyrocketed. She spent half of the night getting to know him.

She was taken back to her adolescence, terrified to see a boy the next day after spending the previous night talking to him nonstop. In Britney's case, things had never gone well. When the boy saw her the next day, he would either ignore her or act as if she was making it up. So she learned to keep her mouth shut about who spoke to her in private.

As she stood on the playground with Noah in tow, she replayed in her mind every text she had sent Dylan. Did she make a move on him? She didn't believe so. Did she say anything that made him uncomfortable? She certainly hoped not. She hoped like hell that things wouldn't be awkward when they came face to face again. What if he mentioned their conversation in front of the other mums and they took it the wrong way?

She didn't care about her own reputation, but she didn't want it to affect Noah in school.

'Britney, did you hear about Cherry Walker?' Liz Beatly yanked her out of her thoughts as she walked towards her with her daughter Isabelle. Britney really didn't know how she put up with this woman on a daily basis. All she wanted to do was gossip, flaunt her wealth, and put people down. Liz was talkative and always found a way to interact with Britney when she was alone, but it was a completely different story when her best friend Jenny was present.

'Asbelle!' Noah laughed as he yanked his hand away from hers and ran over to hug Isabelle.

'No, I didn't hear anything,' Britney replied, still trying to catch her nerve at seeing Dylan.

'Well, she smacked Jenny in the face at The Blue Bell yesterday. She's apparently good friends with that Rosie Forrester,' she gossiped.

Britney sighed and rolled her eyes. She didn't care about any of this, and she had no idea why Liz was even telling her in the first place. Fortunately for her, the whistle blew across the playground as the school doors opened. She took Noah's hand in hers and walked into the school and towards his classroom. Her lungs felt like they were about to collapse, so she took a deep breath. The churning anxiety in her stomach was making her nauseated. *Please don't be awkward, please.*

'Hello, Britney,' a soothing voice said, interrupting her internal panic attack.

Dylan was standing outside the classroom door with a slight smile on his face. 'Are you okay?' he asked, his concern echoed in his gaze. Her heart was thumping in her chest. She'd only known this man for about a week and a half. So why did he have such a strong effect on her?

She mumbled, 'I'm fine.'

'Mr. Coll! I had fun at the park with you yesterday. Are you coming with us again?' Noah interrupted.

Britney wanted to die of embarrassment. Not only did she not know how Dylan would react, but Noah said it a bit too loud for her liking.

'Of course, I will,' he said to Noah before he moved his gaze to meet hers. 'If that's what you want.'

'Yes, it is,' she admitted with a shy smile.

'Dylan, did you hear about Cherry Walker?' Liz Beatly rudely interrupted as she came bombarding down the corridor.

He rolled his eyes. 'No. Anyway, I must be getting back to the kids.'

'Oh, okay. Go in, Isabelle,' she said as she practically shoved her daughter into the classroom before turning back towards them. 'Good God, Britney, how could you come out in public like that? I can't believe I didn't notice that earlier,' she exclaimed, horrified.

Britney felt sick. Noah had accidentally spilled his juice on her crème jumper earlier, and she didn't have time to change because she was rushing out the door. She was so caught up in her nerves at seeing Dylan that she'd completely forgotten about it. 'Noah had a little accident earlier, and I was rushing out the door. I'm not due in the salon for another few hours. So I have time to go home and change.' She had no idea why she felt the need to explain herself. Maybe it was because Dylan was still staring at her.

Liz let out a small chuckle before she walked off.

'You're still beautiful, you know. Don't let her make you think any different.' Dylan spoke softly as he quickly reached out and tucked a strand of hair behind her ear. She was struck. The warmth that flowed through her body lit her up. His piercing blue-green eyes drew her in. She glanced at his soft, inviting lips before he cleared his throat. 'I have to go. I'll text you later, though, and maybe we can all meet up again at the park soon,' he said before turning and walking into the classroom.

She needed to get it together, but first things first. She needed to get home and change her top.

Chapter Nine

MALLS

'LET'S GO SOMEWHERE OTHER than The Blue Bell tonight. I really don't want to run into Jake,' Sarah said as she applied the last of her eyeliner.

'Agreed. Plus, that bitch Cherry practically lives in there,' Brooke huffed as she reached for her black purse, which was propped up against the side of Sarah's sofa.

'What exactly is the problem between you two?' Sarah asked. Brooke and Cherry had never been friends, but lately, the animosity between them had ramped up rapidly.

'She's a stuck-up bitch,' Brooke grumbled. Sarah was sure it was more than that and that it had something to do with Ryker, but every time she tried to pry, Brooke simply shut her down.

They were getting ready for a night on the town. Finally, something that had been long overdue.

'Wanna go to Malls?' Brooke asked, changing the subject—something she excelled at when confronted with a touchy subject. Malls was the town's only cocktail bar. Drinks were pricy, but it was less likely to get rowdy in there after one too many, unlike The Blue Bell.

'Why not?' Sarah said as they walked out of her apartment, ready for the night ahead. Fortunately, Malls was only a couple of streets away, and with these heels, she wasn't up for much walking.

The cold, frosty air hit her as soon as she stepped outside. Her eyes watered slightly, and she hoped her eyeliner hadn't already smudged. She shivered as they approached the bar.

'I told you that you should have worn a coat.' Brooke chuckled. 'Style over comfort? No, thanks,' she said, snug as a bug in her giant bubble coat, jeans, and boots. Sarah was wearing a new dress she had purchased earlier and black strappy heels, and her hair was in perfect waves down her back.

'What kind of music is this?' Brooke scoffed as soon as they walked into the bar. Soft classical music buzzed through the air. Sarah thought it was a relaxing way to start the night, but Brooke wasn't impressed. 'Kelly, what's going on with the music?' Brooke asked one of the girls behind the bar.

'The guy in the corner has taken over the jukebox. I told Merriam we should have gotten rid of that years ago.' Kelly rolled her eyes.

'Well, we'll see about that,' Brooke said as she stomped over to it.

Sarah looked around the room and came to a halt when she noticed who was sitting in one of the corner booths. Hot, irrational anger flooded her. *One. Two. Three. Four.* She dashed to the bathroom. She needed a minute to calm down. She was about two seconds away from causing a scene. She placed her hand on the bathroom counter and took a quick look in the mirror. She could see the tint of red from here. She wanted to punch something—no, someone. She closed her eyes after taking a couple of deep breaths.

'What's wrong?' Brooke cut in as she waltzed into the bathroom.

'He's here!' Sarah snapped, gritting her teeth, 'and he's not alone.'

'Wait, what?'

'Jake is here. He's sitting in the corner booth with that new bartender from The Blue Bell!' Sarah didn't know why she was so angry. As soon as she locked eyes on them, she needed to get out of that room before she did something she would regret. She had good reason to be angry at Jake after what he did, but the rage that ran through her body wasn't just from seeing him; it was from seeing him with another woman. Which was fucking ridiculous, because she hadn't been with him in over ten years.

'You knew you were bound to run into him again. It's a small town. Come on, let's just grab a drink and ignore them,' Brooke said as she reached for her hand to guide her out of the bathroom.

Sarah spent the next hour trying not to look at the other side of the room. Luckily enough, as the night went on, the bar became more crowded, so even if she had wanted to look over, her view would have been blocked.

Keith and a couple of his friends had joined them not too long ago. They were all laughing at one of Keith's many outrageous stories when she felt a prickling sensation on the back of her neck, as if she were being watched. Sarah spun around quickly, only to be met by piercing green eyes staring back at her. She gave him a quick glare before averting her gaze. Why was he looking at her like that? He was the one who'd fucked up all those years ago, not her. Yet she could still feel his eyes on her. Finally, she turned back towards him and mouthed 'What?' in anger. As he moved his gaze to Keith's arm, which was resting at the back of her chair, his glare darkened. *Oh, so that was his issue?* Sarah raised an eyebrow and shifted her gaze to Jake's *date* before returning it to Jake.

He jumped to his feet and muttered something to the woman across from him; she immediately jumped up and grabbed her coat, and they walked straight to the door. Before they left, he shot Sarah one last glare.

· · · ● · ● · · · ·

SARAH FELT ROUGH; PERHAPS going out last night hadn't been such a good idea after all. Not only was the hangover a killer, but she was now stuck here helping Dylan decorate his new apartment. She couldn't really complain because it was her idea in the first place. She hoped he appreciated it because it was time away from the café, but she also knew that if she hadn't offered, he would have left his apartment empty and dull, with no effort to make it a home. Rather than having him pack and leave for another country as soon as possible, she wanted him to have a place that felt like home.

She was curious about how Brooke was holding down the fort at the café. She was worried because it was her first day away from it. She trusted Brooke, but that didn't stop her from imagining the worst-case scenario.

'Dylan. DYLAN. Would you get off that phone of yours and help me move this sofa?' Sarah yelled, failing miserably at her attempt to move it on her own.

'Sorry.' Dylan leaped to his feet, locked his phone, and slipped it back into his pocket before sprinting over to help her.

'Who are you texting anyway? You haven't put that phone down for longer than five minutes since I've been here,' Sarah huffed as she put all her energy into moving the sofa.

Once the sofa was moved to the correct spot, Dylan turned to Sarah and mumbled, 'Just a friend. And you're one to talk. In the last two hours, you have called Brooke non-stop to check in.'

'Sure, just a *friend* who you are constantly distracted by, while I'm left sorting your flat out on my own. And it's not been nonstop at all. I want to make sure everything is running well. We have a delivery due today. Pete and Mark are so rushed off their feet in that kitchen,' Sarah responded as she gave him a stern look.

'I know the café means a lot to you, but it's okay to take a break, you know. Brooke can hold the fort for a day or so. How about we get some food at that new place across town?' Dylan asked.

'The new fried chicken place? Oh, how you spoil me.' Sarah snorted.

'I'm on a teacher's salary. So what do you expect, the Ritz?' Dylan scoffed.

Sarah chuckled as she grabbed a hair tie from her wrist and shoved her long dark hair into a bun.

'No, Ben, you're wrong. When are you coming home, anyway?' A booming female voice could be heard from outside the door. 'I haven't seen you in over—'

Sarah's heart dropped. *Oh no, it's Satan, it's the devil in disguise ...*

'Hello, Mother.' Dylan interrupted Sarah's thoughts and swung the front door open, greeting their mother, Charisse Colling.

Charisse was a tall, slender woman. She was beautiful once, with her long blond hair and blue eyes, but the years had not been kind to her. 'I just got to Dylan's. I will call you later,' she said as she hung up the phone. Sarah knew it was her father, based on what she had overheard. Sarah couldn't recall when she'd last seen him. There wasn't much to say about him because he was so distant. She felt as if she didn't know the man at all. He was never around. Always away on business, or whatever it was he was up to. Even when she was a child, she was lucky if she saw him five times a year. He was a surgeon with his own practice here in town, but that didn't stop him from gallivanting around the world, trying to help everyone who wasn't his own flesh and blood, while his employees ran his surgery and held down the fort here.

'Dylan, I thought I'd just stop by because if I waited for an invitation, I'd never get to see the place,' their mother grumbled, giving Dylan a stern look.

'Yes, well, here it is!' Dylan responded awkwardly, rubbing the back of his neck.

'Hmm, needs some work, but it will do—' Charisse started before she noticed Sarah next to the new sofa. 'Oh, I didn't see you there.'

'I'm just helping Dylan decorate his flat,' Sarah responded as she thought about that fried chicken Dylan promised her earlier. *I bet I'm not going to get it now.*

'Dylan, why didn't you ask me to help you? I'm sure I would be a lot more helpful than Sarah here,' Charisse stated before turning her attention to Sarah. 'No offence, but your style is not up to par with mine,' she said flatly.

Bitch, Sarah thought as she rolled her eyes. This was just one of the reasons Charisse's children tried to avoid her. *Well, the ones that still spoke to her anyway.* She snorted.

'I'm fine with Sarah's help, Mum. You actually just caught us at an awkward time. We were about to go out and grab some food,' Dylan explained as he tried to shoo her back out the door.

'Great, I'll come with you. I've been meaning to see Sarah's little café, but I've not had the time. We can go there now,' Charisse said as she turned towards the door.

How the hell am I meant to get out of this one? Sarah attempted to make eye contact with Dylan, who grunted and walked behind their mother. *It looks like he's no help either. God help me.*

···•·•·••···

SARAH STOMPED INTO TERRANCE Café and spotted the back of a tall blond man in a suit. *One, two, three ...* Her heart immediately took a nosedive to her stomach.

'You wanted me to meet you here in public.' Sarah grinned nervously.

'I'm done sneaking around. I want to be with you, and I can't keep it a secret anymore,' Jake started as he leaned down so his forehead was touching hers. 'The fact that you're here proves to me that you don't either.'

'I love you. I don't care anymore who knows it. What can my mum do? Disown me? I'll deal with that, as long as I get to be with you.' She leaned up slightly and softly kissed him.

A couple of Sarah's classmates walked by and stared before they began to giggle and whisper between themselves. Sarah drew back from Jake's lips and turned towards them.

'Yes, he's my boyfriend. Go and tell whoever you want. I don't care anymore—' she started before Jake's lips cut her off.

When the blond man turned around, she was jolted out of the memory. It wasn't Jake. She had been doing this ever since he came back. Every tall blond man she passed on the street reminded her of him. It had her constantly on edge.

Brooke, who had just finished taking an order for a customer, looked at her in confusion before she glanced behind Sarah and noticed Dylan and Charisse walk in behind her; her face changed to a grimace as she met Sarah's eyes.

'Help me,' Sarah mouthed from across the room. Brooke immediately burst into laughter and then stopped abruptly as she put on a fake cough to cover it up, but Sarah noticed and sent her a glare in response. Brooke smirked before she turned towards her latest customer and took their order.

'It's a bit small. Couldn't you have gotten anywhere bigger, Sarah?' their mother asked snottily, her nose in the air as if she smelled something foul.

'It's a café, Mum, not a large restaurant. It's a perfect size,' Sarah defended as she rolled her eyes. Why couldn't her mother, for once in her life, compliment her success instead of trying to find a way to bring her down?

'Why don't we all just sit by a booth in the window?' Dylan interrupted as he tried to keep the peace, like he always did when she was younger. Sarah cracked a grin. Even though it may sound ridiculous to some, his interruption reminded her so much of the openly loving person he used to be. Not that he didn't love his family; he just had a hard time expressing himself these days.

They all walked over to the booth in question and sat. Brooke dashed to the front of the booth, clutching a notepad and a pen.

'Hey, Sarah, Dylan ... Mrs. Colling. Are you eating today?' she asked.

'Good God! Give us a minute to get our bearings,' Charisse said with a deathly glare.

Brooke was yet another person whom Charisse despised. She saw Brooke as someone who frequently mooched off Sarah. However, Brooke had gotten used to the treatment. After all, it did start when she was six years old, and Charisse had learned that Brooke's father was a factory worker on the other side of town and that her mother worked part-time in a sweet shop near their school.

'We will have three coffees, please.' Sarah looked up at Brooke before mouthing, 'Sorry.'

Brooke smiled before she fled from Charisse's withering glare to start on the coffees.

'Will you stop being so rude to my best friend?' Sarah mumbled. This was precisely why she avoided her mother like the plague and never went to see her. She had a lot more to say to Charisse, but she didn't want to draw attention to herself or start anything that would make her place of business look bad. If they were in Sarah's home, she would tell her mother that she had had enough of her shit and was sick of her attitude, but she had to sit and grit her teeth for the time being.

'I can tell *their* lot has rubbed off on you, with your language alone. I am your mother. Do not talk to me like that,' Charisse whispered with a harsh glare.

Sarah gave her a stern look. She wasn't even going to respond because she knew she'd snap, and she was not about to let her place of business suffer due to her mother. If she could, she would tell her that Brooke and *their* lot, as her mother referred to them, were far better people than Charisse could ever be. Oh, how she wished they hadn't come here. Then she could have really let her mum have it.

'How about some scrambled eggs and toast? That sounds good, right?' Dylan jumped in as he attempted to divert the tension and conversation elsewhere.

'Yes, let's have that,' Sarah replied quickly before glancing back towards Brooke and beckoning her back over.

Brooke quickly brought the coffees to the table and took their food order before walking away.

'So, Dylan, how is the new job treating you?'

'Yes, it's good. The—' Dylan started.

'What the hell is she doing here?' Charisse hissed as she abruptly cut her son off. Clearly, she didn't want anyone else to hear her remark except the people present at the table. She would never embarrass herself in public in such a way. Sarah and Dylan followed Charisse's their gaze to the front door. The surprise on their faces would have been amusing if it hadn't been such an awkward moment—because none other than Britney Adamson had walked into Terrance Café.

Dylan jumped out of his seat and walked over to her before his mum could intervene.

'What is he up to? Why is he talking to that homewrecker?' Charisse mumbled her displeasure.

'He teaches her son,' Sarah responded for the first time since their argument.

'She has the nerve to send her son to a school around here.'

'Well, where else is she meant to send him? You do realise we all live in the same town, right? No matter how much you would like to think that the two different areas are in their own bubbles.' Sarah snorted.

'How are you not more upset about this? This woman seduced the perfect man and ruined your relationship,' Charisse responded harshly.

'The perfect man? You must be joking. Ian was an absolute arsehole. I'm actually glad that what happened back then did happen, as it opened my eyes to what a fake wanker he really was.'

Charisse was convinced that Ian was the perfect fit for her daughter, but this was mainly due to her own high hopes and social aspirations. Ian was a Hennering, which meant something to Charisse. He was the son of one of the town's wealthiest families. His father, William, was always away on business, much like Sarah's father. Still, in his absence,

Ian's mother, Jill, had bought half the stores in town with her husband's money, making her and some of the other women in her mothers' group believe she was above everything and everyone else. Even after everything that had happened, Sarah's mother and Jill remained friends.

Dylan had started walking back to the table, with Britney trailing behind him.

'How dare you even show your face here,' Charisse sneered in a hushed tone as soon as Britney was close enough to the table.

Britney ignored her and looked directly at Sarah once she was at the front of the table. Sarah's shock was obvious. She could feel it was all over her face. She couldn't even hide it; she didn't know what to do or say at that moment. She sat back and hoped Britney would say whatever she needed to say.

'Hello, Sarah,' Britney whispered awkwardly.

'Hi,' Sarah squeaked.

'Could I speak to you privately for a minute?' Britney asked, a desperate expression on her face.

'Now, you just wait a minute. What gives you the right to come in here and demand to speak with my daughter in private after what you did? You are repulsive. The shame—' Charisse huffed quietly in rage, her face flushed. Sarah noticed Charisse look around the café to see if anyone was staring at them. She rolled her eyes as she watched the action. The same old mother, checking to see if anyone she knew was listening in.

'Shut up, Mum. This is none of your business,' Sarah cut her off before turning back to Britney and scooting out of the booth to stand up. 'Sure, we can go over to the empty spot in the corner,' Sarah replied as she walked to another small private table on the opposite side of the café. Britney trailed close behind her.

Sarah looked at Britney once they were both seated across from each other. This was the first time they'd ever been this close in person. Britney was stunning in an innocent sort of way. She had a cute face—the classic 'girl-next-door' appearance.

'I just wanted to come here and apologise to you face to face, finally. I'm so sorry if coming here is awkward, but I didn't know how else to reach you, and I thought this would be better coming from me in person. It's something I should have done years ago, but I didn't have the guts to approach you, and I sent you a letter instead ...' Britney took a deep breath. 'I honestly didn't know you and Ian were still together. When I first met Ian and started getting to know him, he told me you had cheated on him, and he was in the process of breaking it off with you. So I didn't know you were still together when I slept with him, and I certainly had no idea you were engaged when I fell pregnant.' She nervously twiddled her thumbs on the table in front of her.

Sarah didn't know how to think or feel. She'd often imagined that when she finally met this woman, she would be angry and bitter because of the public humiliation that had befallen her after everything had come to light, but instead, she felt relieved. Thankful that she was given the opportunity to see what Ian was really like before making the worst mistake of her life and marrying him.

'Didn't you ever question where he was going? Or where he was staying most nights? We lived together. How could you not know?'

'He would always have me meet him at his friend Tony O'Hara's house. He told me he was staying there until he found a new place. Tony had a tiny apartment, so I never questioned anything when he never asked me to stay over.'

Tony, that stupid bastard, always hated me. 'Tony despised me and was always covering for him. So this comes as no surprise to me. When I was trying to figure out what was going on after Ian left, Tony just ignored my calls and avoided me—before I found out about you, of course.'

'I'm sorry for the part I played in what happened—' Britney started.

'It wasn't your fault. You said you didn't know, and I believe you,' Sarah interrupted her.

She wanted to move on from this. She'd stopped blaming Britney for everything a long time ago, after receiving Britney's letter. Ian was the only person she blamed for what had happened. She wasn't going to let the arsehole cause any more trouble or drama. She was done with it all. He wasn't worth any of it.

'If you want to ask me anything about what happened back then, please do,' Britney mumbled as she glanced down at her hands on the table and played with her fingernails.

'Look, what happened with Ian was actually a blessing in disguise. It kept me from making the biggest mistake of my life and marrying him. It showed me what a fake and a scumbag he truly was.' Sarah sighed.

'I have to go and get my son. I asked one of my colleagues to watch him for half an hour while I made the trip here.' Britney jumped up from the booth. 'Thank you for listening. If you ever want to talk more, Dylan has my number.' She smiled before walking off.

Why would Dylan have her number?

Brooke ran over to Sarah once she noticed Britney had left the café.

'What was that about?' Brooke asked.

'She just apologised to me about Ian.'

'Oh, wow. I knew about the letter, but I never thought she would seek you out,' Brooke said before another customer interrupted and shouted her over. She smiled at Sarah before she hurried off towards the table.

Sarah walked back to the table where her mother and Dylan were seated.

'How did it go?' Dylan asked eagerly.

I'm not sure why he's so concerned about our conversation, but whatever. Sarah slid back in the booth and braced herself for another tongue lashing from her mother.

Chapter Ten

IAN

EIGHT YEARS AGO

SARAH WAS FED UP with being dragged around like a show pony by her mother in order to impress potential investors. So here she was again, dragged to yet another restaurant to *make an impression* with a potential investor's son. Sarah often wondered why, at the age of twenty, she allowed her mother to talk her into these situations. But, on the other hand, she knew she'd never hear the end of it if she didn't comply.

'Don't embarrass me tonight! I want you to make a good first impression because Jill is bringing her son, who has just moved to town. You have no idea how much this could benefit your father,' Charisse whispered into Sarah's ear as they entered the restaurant.

As they walked inside, Charisse examined Sarah, ensuring there were no creases in her clothing and that not a single hair was out of place. Charisse took pride in her perfectionism and expected the same from her daughter.

'Charisse, over here!' a voice called from a small booth in the restaurant's back corner.

Jill Hennering was a tiny dark-haired woman who was beautiful but phony from head to toe. Her beauty was beginning to fade as she grew older. William, her husband, was a wealthy real-estate agent who was considering investing in Sarah's father's private surgery in town. Charisse's mission for the night was to connect with Jill and, in turn, for Sarah to make a good impression on Jill's son, whom they heard was around her age.

'Remember what I told you,' Charisse nagged quietly as they approached the booth.

Sarah sighed and rolled her eyes. She was hoping for a quick dinner so she could get home and binge-watch that new TV show she had recently become invested in.

'Hi, Jill, I'm so glad you could make it.' Charisse smiled sweetly as she shifted her personality on the fly.

'The pleasure's all mine. This is my son, Ian.' Jill smiled as she extended her arm to the man sitting across from her.

Sarah cast a quick glance over at the dark-haired man with gorgeous blue eyes.

'This is my daughter, Sarah,' Charisse introduced as she pushed Sarah into the booth next to him.

Sarah turned awkwardly to face Ian.

'So, what brings you to town? My mum told me you're moving here?' She cracked a grin.

'Yes, a fresh start and all,' he replied with a smile.

'So, Charisse. You have three children?' Jill probed as she snapped her fingers at the server, ordering a bottle of red wine and requesting menus.

Charisse froze on the spot. She despised it when people mentioned her three children because she and Sarah's twin brother, Ryker, didn't even speak anymore.

'Yes ... Dylan, my eldest, is living down south. He got married a couple of months back. It was a lovely ceremony.' Charisse sighed softly.

Lovely ceremony, indeed, except for how Ryker and their parents went out of their way to avoid interacting the entire time—which was extremely awkward because they were all seated together throughout the ceremony and reception. They didn't approve of Ryker's lifestyle or his business, which, to be honest, Ryker couldn't give a shit about. They cut him out of their lives after a major squabble a few years ago. Sarah didn't know the full details of what went down back then because none of them had ever discussed it.

'So, Sarah, where are the best places to go in town?' Ian asked as he tried to pull her attention back to him.

'Why don't you show Ian some of the local places around here? I'm sure you can make it sometime soon, right, Sarah?' Charisse asked sternly as she faced Sarah head on with a hard glint in her eye.

'Sure, we could meet tomorrow if you like.' Sarah smiled at him.

'Okay,' he said, reaching into his jacket pocket and pulling out his phone. He unlocked it and handed it to her. 'Give me your number, and I'll call you to arrange a time tomorrow.' He smirked.

He is handsome, but I have a feeling that he already knows that about himself. Sarah thought as she typed her number into his phone and handed it back to him.

'Let's get our food order in,' Jill said as the waitress returned to the table with the large bottle of wine and took her small notepad from her front pouch.

· · • • • · • • · ·

SIX YEARS AGO

SARAH SLAMMED HER—AND her fiancé's—front door shut in a rage. Ian had just told her he would be working late again tonight. Sarah was suspicious because he'd been working late a lot lately. He would frequently leave the room to make private phone calls, and he also changed the passcode on his phone. They had been together for two years and had been engaged for six months. Their relationship progressed quickly, but everyone was happy about it, from her parents to his family. Sarah's brothers didn't like Ian much, but they were polite to him for her sake. Dylan was convinced that Sarah had rushed into her relationship with Ian without thinking things through, while Ryker thought that Ian was an egotistical, stuck-up prick.

She cooked herself some food and called Brooke for a catch-up. Brooke was currently working at a small pub a couple of streets away and had not long finished her shift when Sarah called her. They chatted for an hour or so before Sarah watched a bit of TV and then had a shower before preparing for bed. She was due an early night as she had a meeting at the bank tomorrow morning. She checked the bedside table clock once she was settled in bed, and it was 11 p.m. She knew Ian was working late, but he had never been this late home before. *Where is he?* she thought before drifting off to sleep, knowing she would most likely see him when she woke up the following day.

The next morning Sarah woke up and turned over in her bed, expecting to see Ian, and noticed his side was empty. She sat up and reached for her phone. *He didn't come home last night. Has something happened to him?*

Sarah: Where are you?

After texting him, she jumped out of bed and began getting ready for the day. After an hour, she still hadn't heard back from Ian, so she tried calling him, but his phone went straight to voicemail. She went to the bank as planned and went about her day as usual. When it was midday, and she still hadn't heard from him, she tried calling him again, but she still had no luck. As the day went on and she still hadn't heard from him, she got worried and called his best friend Tony to see if he had heard from Ian at all. On the first call, Tony's number just kept calling out. On the second call, it didn't call at all. *That prick blocked my number,* Sarah thought in anger, more suspicious than ever. Later that night, she got back to the apartment, and he still wasn't home. She called her frantic mother to see if she had heard anything from Jill, who refused to disclose any information about his whereabouts.

As Sarah lay in bed that second night alone after not hearing from Ian for almost two days, she thought, *why am I not more bothered about this? When Jake left with no warning, I wouldn't get out of bed for weeks, but now with Ian gone, I haven't felt the need to count or calm my anxiety once.* Sarah couldn't understand why she wasn't more heartbroken over this. She was hurt, and she despised the feeling of abandonment, but she could still function normally. Her heart ached, but only a small portion of it appeared to have cracked. Nothing compared to the agony she'd felt the first time someone she'd cared about abandoned her.

She checked her phone when she woke up the next day. Still, there was no response from Ian, and Jill was ignoring her messages entirely. Jill, she had a feeling, knew precisely where Ian was. So she called Brooke to tell her what was going on and asked her to keep an eye out for him. She had never checked in on Ian or asked others to do so before, but desperate times called for desperate measures.

Despite Ian's disappearance, Sarah went to work, saw friends, and asked people to keep an eye out for his whereabouts. Then, after about a week, Sarah received a missed call from Brooke, followed by a text message.

Brooke: Call me ASAP. It's about Ian.

Sarah called right away.

'Sarah? Are you sitting down?' Brooke asked quickly.

'What is it?' Sarah asked softly as she slowly slid down onto the sofa.

'So, I've just finished my shift. I was asking around about Ian. Keeping an eye out for any information on his whereabouts, you know?'

'Yes? What is it? Brooke, spit it out. I know you. I can tell when you're stalling.'

'I was halfway through my shift when one of the regulars, Melanie Adamson, came stomping into the pub demanding double vodkas and shouting her mouth off to anyone who would listen that she had just found out her eighteen-year-old daughter had been knocked up.'

'What does this have to do with Ian?' Sarah asked.

'Well, she claimed that the guy who knocked her daughter up ... is Ian.' Brooke sighed.

'What? This has to be a joke, right? Are we sure she wasn't just talking out of her arse, or she got him confused with someone else?' *Would Ian really cheat on me and get someone else pregnant in the process?*

'Melanie is a loudmouth and a drunk, but she was far too worked up to be lying.'

'Who's her daughter? Have you ever met her?' Sarah probed as she fiddled with a sofa cushion.

'No, she's never been in before, but from what I have heard from Melanie, she's called Britney.'

'Do you know anything else? When he started seeing her? Was it a one-off? Anything...?' Sarah mumbled, desperate to find out more about what was going on.

'Nothing, I'm sorry. Unfortunately, I didn't get a chance to ask before she got thrown out yet again for starting a fight with one of the other women in there.'

'I'm going to go. I'll talk to you later,' Sarah muttered before hanging up the phone.

How could he do this to me? Am I not enough? Why does every guy I care about leave me without a word? Sarah sat dwelling in her thoughts. Knowing she had to tell her parents what happened. Knowing her mother would somehow try to turn this situation around to blame it on her, as Ian could do no wrong in her mother's eyes. Ryker and Dylan would side with their sister, though. *Shit, I'm going to have to get Ryker to calm down and back off before he goes after Ian personally and does some serious damage.* Sarah groaned. Ryker never liked Ian to begin with, so it would be easy for Sarah to ask him to take care of Ian, but for some reason, Sarah didn't want that. She just wanted to move on. Even though the thought of telling people what had happened embarrassed her to no end, she would move on and concentrate on her dream of saving up for the café she wanted.

The shock of the situation was still new, but the more it settled, the less it hurt. *What does this mean?* she asked herself. *Why am I more upset about having to tell my parents and other people in my life about the situation than I am about the actual situation itself?*

Sarah carried on the next couple of weeks like usual. Telling her mother about the situation was hideous. She had a complete meltdown and blamed Sarah for not keeping him occupied and blamed Britney Adamson for seducing Ian in the first place. Charisse blamed everyone apart from the person who was at fault: Ian. Dylan called Sarah a couple of times to let her know he was always there for her and that she could come and stay with him and his wife, Melissa, whenever she wanted to get away from the gossip around town and their parents.

Sarah was correct in her assumptions regarding Ryker. When he found out what happened, he blew up and said he would find Ian and get a couple of his so-called *boys* on the case. Sarah immediately tried to calm him down and begged him not to retaliate; she just wanted it all left in the past and to move on. Plus, she knew bits of what Ryker was capable of and wouldn't wish that on her worst enemy. Ryker didn't react as strongly when Jake left years before, but Sarah often assumed that was because Ryker was slightly hurt; one of his closest friends had left without a word, so he and Sarah both avoided all conversation about Jake. Ian, on the other hand, was a completely different story. It took a lot of begging and pleading for Ryker to leave it alone.

Sarah sat alone on her sofa, drinking a glass of red wine and reading a new book she had bought for herself earlier to distract her from her current situation. When a loud thump interrupted her, she placed her book on the sofa next to her and went to the front door, where the thump had come from. When she looked down, she noticed a letter addressed to her.

Most likely, another "I'm sorry about what happened to you" letter, she thought as she picked it up. So many of her neighbours or people in town kept sending her letters, wishing her well after hearing about the situation. The way they were reacting, you'd think Ian had died. She opened the letter and came to a halt as she began to read. She didn't know how to process the words written on this piece of paper, but she could process the bottom of the letter, where it stated, ***I'm sorry, I didn't know; Take care, Britney Adamson.***

Chapter Eleven

BAYNOR BOWL

PRESENT DAY

THERE WAS A LOUD knock on Britney's front door. She cast a glance at her son, who was busy playing with a toy truck on the living room carpet. She jumped up, walked over to it, and swung it open. Dylan stood there with a large box and a barely visible smile on his face.

'Can I come in?' he asked.

During the last few weeks. Britney and Dylan had been practically inseparable in their free time. It began with a lot of back-and-forth texting, which progressed to long phone calls after a few days. She couldn't stop smiling because she felt so at ease with this man and was able to share her thoughts with someone—other than her son—who seemed to be interested in what she had to say. She appreciated having someone to talk to. Someone to call and talk about her day with, complain about a bad client at work with, and talk about music, art, books, and the world with.

She'd never had anything like that before. Not even when she thought she was dating Ian. He'd just made everything about him, and because she was blinded by him at the time, she didn't see anything wrong with it. Dylan was different. He listened, he inquired; he was intrigued by her. She liked having his friendship. Every day when she picked up Noah from school, she saw him, and they exchanged polite conversation and shy, barely-there smiles. They had only met up a couple of times at the park. This was the first time she had invited him round to the flat. She knew she was very attracted to him, but she didn't want anything to mess up the progress and friendship they had started to build.

'Yeah, come in,' she said as she flung open the door and let him in. A few days ago, she ended up telling him over text about how she finally wanted to confront her past and apologise to Sarah face to face. Funnily enough, he was actually with Sarah that same day. She knew they were planning to stop by the café as he was messaging her during Sarah's visit. So, after some convincing from Dylan's end, she finally worked up the courage and stopped by the café on her lunch break. She was glad she did, as it felt like an enormous weight had been lifted off her shoulders.

As he walked into the flat, he softly moved his hand down her side. Her entire body tingled as butterflies flitted around in her stomach. She took a deep breath before closing the door behind him and walking back into the living room, him close behind her.

'What's in the wrapped box?' she asked.

'Oh, yeah!' He walked over to Noah and sat down on the carpet. 'Look at what I've got for you, little man,' he said as he handed Noah the box to unwrap.

'Presents!' Noah jumped in excitement as he ripped the wrapping paper off the box, then squealed in delight as he turned to face his mum. 'Mummy, look! It's a new Lego set!'

He poured the entire box on the floor and began playing. Dylan gave a small smile before standing and playfully messing Noah's hair up with his hand. He smiled at Britney as he walked over to the sofa and sat next to her.

'Thank you. He loves it,' she gushed.

They sat and made small talk while Noah played with his new Lego set. Her entire body heated up when she felt him reach over and place his hand on top of hers. She flipped her hand over, palm to palm, and slid her fingers between his. He looked over at her before clearing his throat, quickly moving his hand away, and turning towards Noah.

'How about you build us a house with your new Legos?'

'Yes! Good idea, Mr. Coll.' Noah giggled.

'I have a thought. How about we all go bowling?' Dylan asked as he looked at her.

'Yes, yes, please, Mummy, can we go?' Noah asked as his bright blue eyes lit up in excitement.

'Fine, go and get your shoes and coat on.'

'Yayyyy!' Noah jumped to his feet and dashed to get his shoes and coat.

'It's Saturday. I hope you're ready for a packed-out place full of screaming kids,' Britney laughed.

'I work at a primary school. So that's nothing new.'

After Noah finished getting ready, they were out the door and on their way to the bowling alley, which was only about a fifteen-minute walk into town. Britney wore a white and blue summer dress and white sandals because despite it being early October, it was a hot day. She was glad that Dylan saw her in something other than jeans and leggings for once.

'Mummy, I'm going to win! I'm going to win!' He was a very competitive little boy.

'I'm sure you are. We both know how bad I am at bowling. Remember last time?' She laughed.

'What happened last time?' Dylan jumped in.

Noah burst out laughing, tilting his head back and recounting to Dylan the story of the time she dropped the bowling ball on her toe and had to go to A&E. 'You are so silly, Mummy,' he lisped between his chuckles.

When they arrived at Baynor Bowl, they were met with screaming children and stressed-out parents chasing them. It was a crowded place. Maybe coming on a Saturday wasn't such a good idea. Britney groaned as she took in the massive waiting line that stretched from the front door to the front desk. Baynor Bowl was a local bowling alley. It had fifteen lanes in total, a snack bar, and a small arcade in the building's corner. It wasn't much, but it was the town's only bowling alley, and everyone was proud of it—especially the screaming, overly excited children.

'Maybe it wasn't such a good idea after all,' Dylan said as he took in the long line.

'Bowling! Bowling!' Noah shrieked in excitement.

Britney laughed. *Well, maybe this was a good idea, after all,* she thought as she took in his little face that had lit up with excitement.

She turned to Dylan when they were close to the front desk.

'I'll go get us some drinks. What are you having?'

'Just get me a Coke, please.'

'Sure. Come on, Noah.' She reached over to grab his hand and walked towards the refreshments stand.

She finally had her and Dylan's drinks in her hands after what seemed like forever, while Noah had his fruit juice.

She walked back to the lanes as she tried to spot Dylan.

'Britney! BRITNEY! Over here!' A booming voice drew her attention to the far end of the lane on her right. Her gaze was drawn to a waving Dylan, who motioned them over.

'Mr. Coll! Mr. Coll!' Noah shrieked as he dashed over to Dylan.

Her heart began to pound in her chest, and her hands began to sweat. She had no idea why she felt so shy and nervous all of a sudden. She walked slowly towards the lane where Noah was chatting loudly without pausing to take a breath.

'I already set us up for two games. I hope that's okay,' Dylan said.

'That's great,' Britney replied with a shy smile before taking a seat in the booth. This was ridiculous, and she needed to snap out of it. She was fine with him fifteen minutes ago. She had no idea why her nerves had decided to act up now.

'Okay, little man, you're up,' Dylan said as he picked up the lightest bowling ball, set up the bowling ramp, and positioned the ball for Noah to push down the lane.

'Imma win! You just watch, Mr. Coll.' Noah grinned broadly, a determined expression on his face. He pushed the ball as hard as he could and stood back to watch it roll down the lane. His bright blue eyes glowed as he turned to face Britney. 'Look, Mummy, look, I pushed the ball,' he said, grinning.

'Look how well you did. Come on, have your second ball.' Dylan drew Noah's attention by placing another ball on the ramp. Noah dashed over, pushed the ball with all his might, and smiled as it rolled down the lane. His eyes widened as all the pins were knocked down. 'I got a spare,' he exclaimed as he jumped up and down.

Britney rushed over and hugged him as she picked him up and tickled him slightly. 'Well done!'

'Come on, Britney, you're up.' Dylan approached her with a glazed expression on his face.

'Mummy is the worst! She'll need that ball pusher more than I do.' Noah snorted loudly.

Britney's face flushed with embarrassment. She didn't usually get embarrassed so easily, but she couldn't stop herself today.

'Is that so? Come here.' Dylan beckoned to her. She jumped to her feet and walked towards him. He drew her in front of him by her waist and handed her the bowling ball as he moved behind her. 'You need to raise this arm,' he said as he lifted her right arm into position. She could smell his seductive, masculine-scented aftershave, which made her weak in the knees as she felt his hot breath on her cheek. 'Watch your feet. Put them into a certain position like this,' he explained as he let her go, and stepped to the side of her to show her his foot position. 'And then swing the ball towards the lane. Give it a bit of a spin.' He took a slow step back from her and turned to look at Noah. 'Now you try,' he said to Britney.

Britney felt tingles up and down her arm from where he had just touched her, and the butterflies in her stomach wouldn't stop fluttering. She hadn't experienced butterflies like this in a long time. She took the ball and did exactly what he showed her, watching it roll down the lane. She grinned happily as she got a strike.

'GO, MUMMY!' Noah cheered as he jumped on top of the booth seat.

'Watch yourself, little man. You don't want to fall off there,' Dylan said as he picked Noah up and put him back down onto the ground.

Britney walked back over to them both, mumbling, 'Thank you' to Dylan.

'You're welcome!' he replied, giving her a soft look. She smiled slightly as she gazed into his eyes.

'I'm hungry!' Noah complained, interrupting the moment as they both turned towards him.

'How about we go and get some food after here? If that's okay with you,' Dylan added.

'Yes, that's fine, but nowhere expensive, okay?' Britney smiled down at Noah.

'It's fine. Honestly, it's on me.'

'Oh, we couldn't possibly—' she started.

'No, my treat. I'll feel offended now if you say no.' Dylan cut her off with a smile.

She took a brief pause in response to the action. When he smiled, his entire face lit up. She'd never seen anything so beautiful in her life. Her heartbeat sped up, and she worried that it might pop out of her chest. The first genuine smile she had ever seen from him, and it was directed at her.

'Thank you,' she said softly before returning her gaze to Noah. 'Okay, after these games, we'll go get some food, okay?'

'Yay!' He grinned and cheered, both arms in the air.

Britney laughed at his reaction before noticing Dylan's soft gaze on her.

'What, do I have something on my face?' she asked in concern.

'No. Nothing, you're fine,' he replied awkwardly before he turned back towards Noah. 'My turn now! So who's going to be crowned king of bowling tonight?' he asked playfully.

'Me, of course, Mr. Coll,' Noah guffawed confidently.

'We'll have to see about that,' Dylan scoffed before reaching for another bowling ball in preparation for his turn.

They continued their two bowling games as normal. As random people walked by and glanced at them, Britney would overhear them remark to one another in hushed tones about what a cute family the three of them made. She knew that when they looked over, all they saw was a loving family with how Dylan acted around Noah and how at ease he was with him.

· · • • • • • • · ·

BRITNEY SAT ON HER sofa drinking a glass of juice as she chatted quietly with Dylan. It had been over an hour since she put Noah to bed. She had a fantastic day, and she knew that Noah did too, as he hadn't stopped beaming since they got back to the flat. After she settled Noah down, gave him his bath, and put him to bed, she relaxed on the sofa with Dylan at her side.

'So, then, Ryker accused me of fancying you.' Dylan chuckled awkwardly after explaining a brief argument he'd had with his brother the day before.

'Why would he think that?' Britney asked. She didn't even know his brother knew about their friendship.

'Well, because Sarah ended up telling him that I had your number and he confronted me about it, so I told him that we're friends,' Dylan said.

'He accused you of fancying me because we're friends?' Britney asked, confused. *Were men and women not allowed to be just friends now?*

'Well, he tried to set me up with one of his fling's—Cherry's—friends. I turned it down because I didn't want to get involved with anyone. He accepted that, and then Sarah asked me about having your number. So he took that as me liking you because you're the only woman I've been speaking to a lot lately and seem to have taken an interest in,' he explained.

Britney noticed a red tint creeping up from his neck and covering his cheeks in embarrassment. She smiled at how cute that was.

'Well, that's ridiculous, right?' Britney murmured as their faces drew closer together.

'What is?' Dylan gulped.

'You know—' Britney began before she was cut off.

Dylan's lips softly touched Britney's—for two beats of her heart—before he abruptly pulled away and dragged himself off the sofa.

'What's wrong?' Britney whispered as she looked up into his soft blue-green eyes. Panic overtook her body right away. She hadn't intended for that to happen. She didn't want anything to change. She wasn't ready for any of this.

Dylan sagged as tears welled up in the corners of his eyes.

Defeated.

Broken.

Britney had never seen anything so captivating in her life. His gentle soul was filled with so much grief that it shone through his eyes. That slight sparkle that was screaming out to love and to be loved again, but not knowing how.

'I don't know how to do this,' he said. 'Melissa's death still haunts me every day. I used to wake up every morning and she was the first thing on my mind. Now when I wake up, somehow over the last few weeks, that changed, and you got in here.' He softly tapped his finger against his temple, looking grave and grief-stricken. 'I'm scared. I can't lose her. I can't live with the guilt that I'm somehow betraying her. I can't give you anything other than friendship, even though a part of me wants to,' he said, reaching out to Britney and softly tucking her hair behind her ear. He turned away and walked slowly towards the door, then walked out of it without looking back, and she let him go.

She didn't know how to do anything else but watch the people she cared for constantly walk out the door.

Chapter Twelve

BROKEN

SARAH STOMPED INTO TERRANCE Café in a foul mood. This had not been her morning at all. First, her alarm didn't go off; she was at least thankful that she didn't have to open up this morning. Then her car wouldn't start—after plenty of cursing—and she had to get the bus, which she hadn't done for years, which resulted in her being stuck sitting next to a man who smelled like he hadn't had a wash in weeks and a teenage girl gossiping loudly on her phone for the entire journey. Plus, with the bad traffic this morning, her mood was completely shot.

'Coming through,' yelled Megan, one of her waitresses, as she carried a large tray full of hot drinks and wispy pieces of her blond hair escaped her bun.

'Good morning, Megan,' Sarah said as she took a step back.

'Good morning, Sarah. As you can see, it's a hectic morning today.' Megan smiled sweetly as she walked past her and towards a table full of customers.

Sarah drew a deep breath and looked around the café. She immediately noticed the back of a blond man and was convinced that her mind was playing tricks on her as it had been doing for weeks, but as soon as he turned and she caught a glimpse of his face, it aggravated her mood even more. Jake stood there chatting with Keith as if he didn't have a care in the world. The rage hit her stomach so hard that she didn't even need to count to calm down. The second she looked at his face, her anger won the battle against her anxiety. He was stood by a small table near the small stage. *What the hell is he doing here? Does he not get it? I don't want anything to do with him, never mind being friends. It looks like my morning just got a whole lot worse.*

Brooke ran over to Sarah after noticing her across the room. She appeared extremely frazzled, with bits of her long, curly dark hair falling out of her ponytail and a deer-in-headlights look in her eyes.

'Thank goodness you're here. It's been hectic, and Becky called in sick!'

'What?' Sarah groaned. 'I'll give Susie a call and see if she can come in earlier and help.'

Susie was one of the café's younger waitresses. She only worked a few hours a week, mostly on weekends because she was only sixteen and went to college during the week.

Great Saturday morning. Sarah groaned. *The busiest time of the week for us, and one of my girls has already called in sick, on top of the awful morning I've had.*

'That would be great, thank you. I've been running around like a headless chicken since I opened up.' Brooke sighed, exhausted. Sarah felt guilty as she looked at Brooke's expression. I should have gotten here sooner, she thought.

'I'm so sorry you and Megan have been left alone for so long. I've had the worst morning, and now I have to deal with him as well.' Sarah nodded in Jake's direction. 'How long has he been here?'

'About twenty minutes, and now that you're here, will you please ask Ryker not to bring his goons in here anymore? They're scaring the other customers,' she grumbled as she looked across the room to where Ryker sat. 'I would ask him myself but he would just laugh in my face, and Megan said she would rather poke her eyeballs out than ask any of them to leave!'

Sarah glanced across the room and noticed that one of the large booths in the café's corner was full. Ryker sat at the front of the booth, arms folded, deep in conversation with the scary-looking goons in question, who were giving harsh glares to everyone in the café who glanced their way.

This is not the place for one of Ryker's meetings. Can't he find somewhere else to take his goons? Sarah huffed as she approached the booth.

'Ryker, can I talk to you for a second alone?' Sarah asked softly, tugging on her brother's arm.

'Sure,' he said as he slid out of the booth. 'Back in a second, lads,' he said to the group as he followed her to the café's corner.

'You know I love you, and I don't mind if you come here, but your cronies are scaring away my customers.' Sarah sighed and begged, 'Please, can you hold your business meetings somewhere else?'

At that moment, another of Ryker's '*employees*,' a local lad named Tom, walked through the café's front door. Sarah groaned. *Not another one.*

Ryker's gaze was drawn to the door.

'No! Wait outside,' he said to Tom in his authoritative tone.

Tom came to a halt, gave a slight nod, then turned and walked straight back out the door. Sarah rolled her eyes as she watched the action. *I'll never understand what power he has over these people. If it's not his crew, it's wealthy investors or even a couple of the officers on the police force. I'm so glad I don't try to figure out precisely what Ryker does. I'm sure I'd be shocked, based on how others treat him.*

'All right, sis. I'll take my meeting elsewhere. I'll see you later.' Ryker said this before turning his head towards the table full of his 'employees' and saying, 'We are leaving. Grab your shit. Let's go!' He walked towards the door, his goons trailing closely behind him.

Sarah returned her gaze to Jake and Keith, who were still chatting and laughing between themselves. *What's so bloody funny? Why is he even here?* Sarah grumbled angrily to herself before stomping over to them.

'So, when are you running back to London, Jake? Or is that now off the cards? What happened? Why did you leave?' Sarah cut herself off as she smirked. 'Well, leaving is something you're good at, isn't it? Was there another girl you just had to run out on?' Sarah taunted. *I've had enough of being civil to this guy. He needs to leave now.*

'Rough morning, then, Sarah?' Keith smirked at her menacing stare.

'Yes, and walking into this place and seeing'—she gave Jake a quick once over—'things that aren't wanted here.' She smirked directly in his face. A cloud of rage overtook his features, and his jaw clenched. *Yes, be mad, bastard.* Sarah's smirk widened.

He finally snapped, tired of all the hostility.

'That's it!' He pulled Sarah softly by the arm before turning towards Keith. 'Excuse us.'

He huffed angrily as he dragged her through the crowded café, flung open the door to the employees-only cloakroom, and pulled her inside with him before slamming the door shut behind them.

'What the hell are you doing? Get off me,' Sarah snapped as she yanked her arm out of his hold.

'What is your problem?'

'Where's your new girlfriend?' Sarah taunted.

'What are you talking about?' Jake snapped.

'The bartender.' *Is he fucking stupid?*

'Louise? I went out with her once, and I haven't seen her since.'

'Well, didn't take you long to bin someone else, did it?'

'I'm sick of your snarky comments! You have such a problem with me being back here? Now's the time to get it off your chest. I'm not putting up with this bullshit anymore. I have gone out of my way to be fucking civil with you! But all you want to do is fight with me or find some way to tear me down. What is it you want from me?' He ran his hand through his short blond hair. A trait he never grew out of, it seemed.

'Fine. You really want to know?'

'Yes!' he barked.

'I want the truth. I want to know why. I want to know why it was so easy for you to throw me away like trash and then skip town without even telling me.'

'You think it was easy for me to leave you?' he snapped as he took a step closer and leaned directly in her face.

'Sure seemed like it. Like it was easy to break up with me over a fucking text.' *How fucking dare he. How dare he act like he was the one who was discarded so abruptly.*

'What, and you think I could have stood in front of you, face to face, and finish with you? Don't be fucking stupid. You know how much I loved you—you know!'

'You loved me so much that you picked a new life in London over me?'

Yeah, he loved me so much that while I cried myself to sleep every night for months, he was living it large down south.

'Don't do that. Don't act like I wasn't on borrowed time.' He shook his head as his green eyes blazed hotly.

'What the hell are you talking about?' Borrowed time? He was the one who'd finished with her. He was the one who'd decided they were better off apart than together.

'I'm talking about how I was never good enough for you. How you always deserved someone better than me. Someone who could give you a better life and a family without having this dark cloud hanging over their head and waiting to screw up at any moment.'

'Jake, I never acted like I was too good for you. I wanted you. I loved you. I wanted a future with you!' She tried to hold back the tears that began to well up in her eyes.

'Oh, please! You and your parents were just waiting to find a way to get me out of your life, and when the opportunity came, they jumped at it so they could carve the way for you to meet someone they approved of. Part of you hated not having their approval. Hated that I couldn't fit into your world!'

'What are you talking about? What do my parents have to do with any of this? I was shattered when you left. I would have picked you over anyone, and deep down, you know that. You ran because you were scared. After all, never in your life had you ever had anything real before, and once you had that, you didn't know what to do with it!'

'I was EIGHTEEN! You have no idea what I had to give up. You have no fucking clue what I was dealing with ... and that was very real!'

'Yes, you were, but so was I, and I knew what I wanted. It's a shame you didn't love me enough to fight for me and pick me like I would have picked you. You broke my heart, and honestly? It's never fully recovered.'

'Don't give me that shit. You don't think I kept track of you over the years? You don't think I know that you got engaged to another guy? Don't you dare try to make out that you were pining away for me.'

'I got engaged because I wanted to get over you, don't you see? So tell me, Jake, after I found out that my ex-fiancé got another girl pregnant and skipped town, why didn't I break? I'll tell you why, because I was already broken when I met Ian. I've been broken since the day you left me.' She sobbed in defeat.

They were too close; Sarah felt his breath on her cheek. She looked up into his piercing green eyes, and then his mouth was on hers, hot and demanding. Everything else faded away—the pain, the heartache, the broken promises. All that mattered in that moment was him and his soft lips that parted hers so easily.

Chapter Thirteen

FRIENDS

BRITNEY WAS HAVING THE worst day. Scratch that. The worst couple of days. She hadn't heard from Dylan since he'd walked out on her the other night. Things had gotten out of hand. She'd always known she was attracted to him, but she hadn't planned on kissing him. She didn't want to complicate her life more than it already was. She didn't date or get involved with anyone after Ian. That kiss with Dylan was her first kiss in five years. All she needed was her son. She couldn't afford to let anyone else in. She knew the pain that came with being abandoned and would not put herself through that again. She would not risk putting her son through the same pain she went through. She did, however, miss her friend. Dylan was the first person she had struck up a good friendship with in such a long time. She missed his quirky texts and the slight smile he gave her when she felt his steel walls were slowly crumbling, which made her heart race. The way he treated her son. His protective instincts.

The deep conversations, his interest in her life. She didn't want a single kiss to change that.

She got worried when he wasn't at school the last couple of days. She could understand his confusion and pain over the entire situation. She knew it would have brought back some painful memories for him. She tried asking the school where he was, but they wouldn't tell her. Her last resort was to ask his sister and considering she didn't have Sarah's number, Britney decided to stop into the café on her lunch break from work while Noah was at school. She knew she would look crazy, but she didn't know what else to do. She wasn't about to lose the first friend she'd had since she was a kid.

Britney arrived at Terrance Café shortly after one on a Wednesday afternoon. As she rushed inside the café, she hoped it wouldn't be too crowded so she could snag a moment with Sarah. She quickly glanced across the room and spotted her serving a customer at the counter.

She took a deep breath to calm herself before walking over.

'Hi, Sarah. Please can I have a second of your time?' Britney asked politely.

'Oh, hi, erm ... sure,' Sarah replied awkwardly before walking over to Britney and asking, 'What's up?'

'I'm sorry to have to ask you this, and I don't want to seem like a total psycho, but'—Britney rushed out without pausing to take a breath—'have you heard from Dylan?' she finished in embarrassment. She couldn't believe she had to resort to asking his family members about his whereabouts.

'I haven't heard from him in a couple of days. Why? Is something wrong?' Sarah's eyes widened in panic.

'I'm not sure. He hasn't been at the school for the last couple of days, and he's not texting me back. Last time I saw him, we weren't exactly in the best place. So please could you just make sure he's okay and let me know?' Britney pleaded.

'Okay, but how would I contact you?'

'Take my number.' Britney pulled her phone from her front pocket and relayed her number to Sarah, who, in turn, took out her own phone and saved it.

'Got it,' Sarah said as she slid her phone back into her front pouch.

'Thank you. I'm so sorry for bothering you. It must feel weird that we have only had one conversation, and I'm already running to you asking after your brother.' Britney nearly choked in embarrassment.

'I'm used to women asking after my brother, but they mostly as for Ryker, not Dylan. Not for a long time, anyway. Well, apart from once, a couple of weeks ago,' Sarah mumbled.

'I don't mean to put you in an awkward position or anything—'

'No, it's fine. Don't worry about it.' Sarah smiled as she cut her off.

'I didn't know who else to ask. I know he pretty much keeps to himself,' Britney began to explain nervously as she looked around the room, catching odd looks from customers.

'Yes, since he's been back in town, he hasn't hung around many people. Can I ask why you're looking for him? I mean, I know he's your son's teacher, and I know he has your phone number, but my question is why? Is there something going on?' Sarah asked.

'He's my friend.' Britney didn't know how else to describe it. She felt like he was so much more than her friend. He was her best friend, someone she'd come to care a lot about, but she knew that would sound strange to say out loud, considering she hadn't known him long at all.

'Oh, okay. It's just you're the first woman I've seen him pay any attention to since the accident.'

'I don't know. I'm sorry. I don't know what to say—'

A loud throat clearing interrupted their conversation, and both women turned to see Crystal Shavis, who was frowning.

'Can I help you?' Sarah asked.

'I have been waiting for my latte for ten minutes. What is taking so long?' Crystal grumbled as she stomped over to the counter.

'I'll be with you in just a second, Crystal,' Sarah replied with a forced smile on her face.

'Good. I do have things to do, you know,' Crystal said. 'Have you seen anything from that Rosie Forrester lately? I told her husband all about her disgraceful behaviour with Keith.' Crystal let out a snort with her nose in the air. She then noticed Britney for the first time. 'Well,' she began as she gave Britney a quick glance and wrinkled her nose in annoyance before turning her attention back to Sarah. 'I'll be waiting for my latte to go.'

Britney gave Crystal a dry look before returning her gaze to Sarah. 'My lunch break is almost over. Let me know how he is?' Britney smiled and walked towards the door before she said anything to that snobby cow Crystal that she might regret in the future, and possibly lose another one of her regular clients at the salon.

· · • • • • • • · ·

BRITNEY HAD JUST FINISHED putting Noah to bed for the night when she heard a loud knock on her front door. She walked over to check the peephole and was taken back when she saw Dylan. She quickly unlocked the door and swung it open.

'Hey,' he said awkwardly as he fixed his gaze on her.

'Hey, come in.' She stepped back to allow him inside and shut the door behind him. She wondered what he was doing here. She hadn't expected to see him. Since that kiss, he hadn't responded to any of her texts or phone calls.

'Look, I'm sorry for not speaking to you over this last week. My head's been all over the place,' he began.

'I get it, I do. What happened shouldn't have happened. It's clear that neither one of us is in any place right now to get romantically involved, but I miss you.' She glanced up at him. 'I miss my friend. I don't want to lose you.'

He took a deep breath and said, 'I miss you too, and you're right. I can't be with anyone right now. I'm not even sure if I can be with anyone again, but that's my cross to bear.'

'I know, and I have Noah! He's my number-one focus; he always will be. Nothing is going to get in the way of that.' She didn't want to let anyone back into her heart or bed, but she wasn't about to tell him.

'I do want to say something to you before we sweep this under the rug. I am attracted to you. I like you, but I haven't been involved with anyone since my wife. You are the first woman who has caught my interest. So I want you to understand that my just wanting to be friends has nothing to do with you. If I met you in another life, I wouldn't hesitate. Trust me.'

She closed her eyes and took a deep breath. She felt the same way. Perhaps things would have been different if she had met him before Ian. Maybe they'd be together, but then she wouldn't have had Noah, and she wouldn't change that for the world. 'I feel the same way.'

'Friends?' He smiled down at her and opened his arms.

'Friends,' she said, falling into his arms and hugging him.

She was glad he was back, even if they couldn't be together. She'd still have him in her life. Friendships, on average, outlasted relationships anyway.

·•••••••••·

IT WAS A BRIGHT, HOT, sunny day, 30 degrees Celsius to be exact, which was unusual for northern England. Particularly at this time of year. Noah was dressed in his favourite football shirt, blue shorts, and his new cap. Britney coated him with sun lotion so his fair skin wouldn't be burnt. Her outfit consisted of a white vest top, blue shorts, and flat black pumps. They were laughing between themselves as they walked up the gravel road towards their usual park, swinging their joined hands back and forth.

'Mummy, look! It's a doggy!' Noah clapped as he squealed in delight at a small dog that ran towards them. Britney laughed at Noah's joy. She loved dogs and would get one if she could take care of it, but she was too busy working and caring for Noah. She lacked both time and energy. It would be cruel not to be able to give a dog the love and attention it deserved.

'Get back here!' yelled an angry voice further up the road. Britney froze; she knew that voice. The hairs on the back of her neck stood up, and her entire body went on high alert. *It couldn't be him, right? Why is he here? Why now?* So many questions raced through her mind. Her breathing became more rapid.

'Mummy, are you okay?' Noah asked, his big blue eyes shining with concern as he looked up at her.

She cast a glance in the direction of the voice. Two figures approached them, not noticing her or Noah for a second. Finally, Britney was able to catch her breath. Her heart dropped into her stomach. She lowered her gaze to Noah. She couldn't do this. How was she meant to tell him? It wasn't the time or place.

'Britney Adamson? Oh, I didn't realise you were still in town. So you're still in that shithole of an estate?'

The devil himself, Ian Hennering, approached them. Ian's face twisted in a grimace as he looked down at the small figure who was confusedly tugging on his mum's hand.

Britney ignored him and tried to walk past, dragging Noah behind her. Ian took a step forward, refusing to let her pass.

When she caught up to them, the tall, pretty redhead with Ian asked, 'What's going on?'

'Nothing. Stay out of it, Anna!' He glared at the woman before returning his gaze to Britney. 'I'm surprised you even kept him.' He scoffed and rolled his eyes as he looked down at Noah.

'Ian ... what?' Anna started.

'Bitch, I told you to stay out of it. What exactly don't you get about that? You think just because you're my wife, you can stick your nose in my business?' he snarled before returning his gaze to Britney. 'Don't expect any money from me. You knew I didn't want that kid, but you had him anyway.'

'Mummy, who are these people?' Noah asked.

This pulled Britney out of her shocked silence, and she finally responded to Ian, 'I don't want anything from you. Now let me past.'

'Kid? Wait a minute ... he's yours? You never told me you have a child.' Anna's gaze was immediately drawn back to Ian.

'I said, SHUT UP!' Ian roared. Anna's entire body jumped in fear as she looked down at the ground.

Britney was gobsmacked by their interaction. She always knew Ian was a piece of shit, but how he was treating his apparent wife in public was shocking. She was afraid of finding out how he treated her in private. Given his reaction when he'd found out Britney was pregnant, it didn't surprise her in the least that he hadn't mentioned Noah to his wife.

'What are they talking about, Mummy?' Noah whimpered in confusion as he shifted his gaze between the adults.

'Nothing. Come on!' she said quickly, pulling Noah behind her as she passed them.

'Who said you can go anywhere?' Ian scoffed as he harshly grabbed hold of Britney's wrist.

'Get off me NOW!' Britney snapped as she yanked her arm from his hold.

'Don't fucking raise your voice to me. You should be thankful that I even let you have that kid. I gave him to you. I could take him away just as easily. Remember that. I'm sure my parents wouldn't mind taking the little shit on,' he threatened.

Britney saw red. How dare he threaten her son like that? How fucking dare he? 'You will never touch him. Do you hear me, you piece of shit?'

'Please, let's just go.' Anna approached Ian from behind and gently placed her hand on his arm in a plea.

'I told you to STOP TRYING TO TELL ME WHAT TO DO!' Ian roared as he elbowed Anna hard in the stomach.

'What are you doing? Leave her alone!' Britney trembled, horrified at what she was witnessing.

Noah burst into tears.

'It's okay, baby!' Britney whispered as she picked him up and attempted to walk away from the situation.

Ian rolled his eyes in irritation before grabbing Anna's wrist and dragging her down the street, their dog close behind. Britney turned back and stared in horror at the display before they vanished around the corner. She didn't know the whole story or what Ian and his wife's relationship was like, but she could take a guess based on that brief interaction. She felt sorry for the woman and hoped she could find the strength and help she needed to get away from Ian before it was too late.

Noah finally stopped crying and wrapped his arms around his mum's neck, hugging and pulling her close. Britney smiled softly at the display before a worried expression took over her face. She didn't know what Ian was up to, but if he came after her son in any way, he would have hell to pay.

Chapter Fourteen

CHARLOTTE

IT HAD BEEN MORE than a week since Sarah lost her mind and kissed Jake. After she'd kissed him in the back room for a few minutes, she realised what she was doing, pulled away, and ran out of the café. When she got a couple of streets away, she sighed and went back, knowing she couldn't just leave Brooke in the lurch like that, given how busy it was that day. He was gone when she returned, and she hadn't seen him since.

Today she was out around town shopping with Brooke, something they hadn't done together in a while, and she thought it was long overdue.

'What about this?' Brooke asked as she held up a black dress off the rack.

'Yeah, it's nice.'

'Okay! Spill. You have been like this all week. Down in the dumps. What's going on?' Brooke sighed before she placed the dress back on the for-sale rack.

'My head is just all over the place. With what happened with Jake, and my mum has really been on my case lately. Oh, and Dickhead is back in town too.'

'Well, for starters, ignore your mum. You know what she's like. As for Ian, I heard about that. Thankfully, I haven't run into the wanker yet,' Brooke said as she glanced over at some new black boots.

'I have nothing to say to him. I haven't for years. He's a manipulative piece of shit, and when Dylan told me he was back, I decided then and there that I wasn't going to let him waste any more of my time. So if I see him, I'm not going to interact or let him get to me in any way. Besides, I have other issues I need to sort out.'

'Yeah, like resolving your issues with Jake,' Brooke said.

'I guess.'

'You should just jump on his dick.'

'Brooke!'

'What? I'm not telling you to marry him, but it's clear you're still into him and he is gorgeous. So why not just let all your frustration out in his bed, or yours, or the against the wall—'

'I get it. I get it.' Sarah cut her off, laughing. Brooke never failed to make her laugh. She just got right to the point with her no-nonsense outlook on life.

'But for real, though, I think you need to sit down with him and discuss everything that's happened in the past, if not for the future, then for closure at least, as you have never gotten over it.'

'I suppose. I just don't know how to approach the conversation because every time I see him, either my anxiety takes over or this anger boils up inside of me. Which was another thing. When I found out that Ian is back, I didn't have any emotion whatsoever about it; it just was.

But with Jake, I just don't know what to think or feel anymore. Every blond guy I pass on the street reminds me of him.'

'You never got over him. I know it, and deep down, you know it too. Consider how different you were when Ian left compared to when Jake left. Jake's departure was as if a piece of you had gone with him.'

'I know.'

'What's going on anyway with Dylan and Britney Adamson? I'm hearing shit all over town about them always being seen together.'

'They are apparently just *friends*, but I think he's into her. He just doesn't want to do anything about it. Which I don't blame him for, after what happened with Melissa.'

'Seriously? Britney Adamson and your brother? That's weird as shit. Aren't you freaked out at all by that?'

'I thought I would be. But it hasn't bothered me at all. Dylan seemed a lot happier these last few weeks, the happiest I've seen him since the accident, and if it's Britney that makes him feel like that, then who am I to judge? No idea what's going on there. He says they're just friends. I don't buy it, but that's their business, I guess—' Sarah cut herself off as some new shoes caught her eye and she pointed at them. 'Oh ... they look nice.'

'As long as you're all right with it, I guess.'

They spent the rest of the day shopping while Brooke tried her hardest to cheer Sarah up.

· • • • • • • • • ·

THERE WAS A LOUD knock on the front door. Sarah groaned as she pulled herself up from the sofa, walked over to her door, and pulled it open.

Ryker was leaning against the door frame, arms crossed, his blue-green eyes sympathetically looking at her. *Why is he looking at me like that?*

'What's up? Why are you looking at me like that?'

'There's something you need to know. I'm not the person to tell you either,' Ryker said.

'What's happened? Is everyone okay? Dylan? Brooke?' Sarah panicked.

'They're fine. Everyone's fine. It's nothing like that. Please just listen to what he has to say and don't freak out before he's explained, all right?'

Ryker looked over his shoulder towards the end of the apartment complex's corridors. Sarah followed Ryker's gaze, and when her gaze locked on *his,* her entire body boiled with rage. *What the fuck is he doing here?* She hoped he hadn't come for round two because there was no way she was kissing him again.

'What the hell is he doing here? What do you think you're doing—'

'Just listen to what he has to say,' Ryker interrupted. 'I'll leave you both to it.' He turned and walked away.

Jake had the audacity to smile at her as soon as they came face to face.

'This had better be good. Come inside before I change my mind.' She took a step back from the door to allow him in.

Once she closed the door, she turned back towards him. 'What? I haven't got all day.'

'I don't even know where to start, but I feel you have the right to know the truth.' He took a deep breath and asked, 'Do you remember my mum and the issues she had?'

'What? Did you really come over here to talk about your mum?' Sarah scoffed.

'Just hear me out.'

'Yeah, I remember you telling me about her addictions,' Sarah said. 'What does this have to do with—'

'Remember how I told you about her pregnancy a few weeks before I left? Well, finding out about Charlotte—my little sister's name—gave her a reason to finally get clean. Granted, I was pissed off because she didn't do it for me,' Jake explained. 'But at the same time, I was relieved that she had finally decided to put her family first. She began applying for jobs and blocked all her dealers' phone numbers. Of course, the baby's father kept coming round to try to talk to her, but she just sent him away because he was no good.'

'I'm glad she finally got clean,' Sarah said softly. She had no idea where this was going, but she felt she was about to find out.

'The night before I left, we had a visitor at the house. She came in and threatened to involve social services and have Charlotte taken away as soon as she was born. They had high-ranking friends and threatened to inform them about my mum's drug addiction. We begged and pleaded with her to give us time to prove my mum could stay clean and care for my sister once she was born. She told us the only way she would leave us alone and not try to take away my sister was if I left town without saying anything and left you—'

He took a deep breath while running his hands through his blond hair and looking down at the floor.

What? Why would someone do that? What kind of person would threaten to take a mother's child just to get Jake to leave Sarah? Who in their right mind would do that?

Sarah paused as a horrifying thought brought her world crashing down around her. She desperately wanted to be wrong, but she knew. Only one person would benefit from it, the one person who despised them being together more than anyone else. Sarah felt a lump in her throat. Her chest was caving in.

'Was it ... my mum?' Sarah asked, distraught, staring down at her hands and avoiding his gaze.

'Yes.' Jake sighed. She felt his green eyes fixed on her. 'I didn't want to leave you. I loved you more than anything. I'd loved you since I was four years old and didn't even understand what love was, but I couldn't put my family at risk. I couldn't risk my unborn sister getting snatched from us at birth. I needed to protect my family. I was put in a tough situation, and it was the most difficult thing I'd ever had to do.'

He stopped and took a step closer to Sarah, cradling her face with his hands and resting his forehead on hers. 'I took my mum down south with me for a few years, helped her stay clean, and made sure Charlotte was well cared for. She eventually wanted to come back here because, despite the fact that this town is messy, small, and full of drama. It's her home. So she moved back with Charlotte. I've kept a close eye on her over the years. She's been doing great. She hasn't had a slip since she found out she was pregnant. I stayed down south after uni, got a good job, got into some trouble, and decided to come back here.'

Jake softly stroked Sarah's face. 'There's more. It's going to be difficult for you to hear this, but it's not my story to tell.'

Sarah closed her eyes. Her heart was pounding so hard that it felt like it was splitting in two. She was certain he could hear it. She wasn't sure if her heart was breaking or if the pain she was experiencing was the result of it healing after finally finding the answers she'd been seeking for so long. 'What else is there?'

'Will you come with me to my mum's? She will explain everything.'

Jake pulled away and headed towards the door. Sarah was still too stunned to speak or react. She felt as if her entire body was frozen, and even the slightest movement would cause her to collapse. *One. Two. Three.* The fact that there was more made her head spin. She took a deep breath and tried to push back the rage that was rising against her mother. Why would she do something like that? She felt sick to her stomach. She knew her mum was a real piece of work, but she clearly hadn't known how much. She had to know what else there was. What did Jake mean when he said it wasn't his story to tell?

Sarah slowly followed him out the door and locked it behind her without making a sound. She didn't cry, but she had to keep her breathing under control. Whatever she was about to learn couldn't possibly be worse than what she had just heard.

· · • • • · • • • · ·

SARAH AND JAKE PULLED up in front of a small two-story house. The outside was worn and in need of a fresh coat of paint and a thorough cleaning. Sarah hadn't seen Cora, Jake's mother, since she was a teenager, and now she was about to sit down with her and talk about the past.

Sarah almost tripped over a pink bicycle as they walked towards the front door of the house. Jake laughed as he reached over to help her regain her balance. 'My mum is always telling Charlotte not to leave her stuff lying around.'

Charlotte was Jake's nine-year-old sister. Another person whom Sarah had yet to meet. It seemed odd that she had such a long history with Jake but had yet to meet the same little girl her mother had threatened. Jake leaned in and rapped on the front door. Sarah was getting nervous, but she was relieved that Cora was expecting them. Even though Jake's call from the car was brief, Britney was glad Cora knew they were on their way.

The front door swung open, revealing a beautiful Cora Cremell. Tall and slender, with long blond hair and Jake's green eyes. She had always been a beautiful woman, but Sarah could see the years were catching up with her. There were wrinkles around her eyes, hard lines around her mouth, and her long blond hair was losing the shine it had when Sarah was a child. Cora smiled at them both and took a step back as she led them into her home.

The inside of the house was small but well kept, a long stretch from the place the Cremells used to live in before they moved down south.

'Jake, it's great to see you. Charlotte hasn't stopped talking about you since your last visit,' Cora said as she took a step forward and hugged him.

'Hi, Mum. You remember Sarah, right?' Jake asked as he took a step back towards Sarah.

'Oh, yes, hello again,' Cora replied nervously before an awkward silence dawned on them.

'Where's Charlotte?' Jake asked.

'She's next door, playing with her friend from school. Let's go into the front room, shall we? I can already tell this will be a heavy conversation,' Cora said as she led them into the small living room, directing them to follow her.

The living room wasn't much to look at: one old, worn-out black sofa, a small TV, and a small wooden table smack dab in the middle of the room. But Sarah felt the warmth as she took in a large plastic blue box in the corner overcrowded with toys, and a small pink beanbag placed next to it. Many of Charlotte's drawings were hung on the wall, each with a date in the bottom right corner, some dating back several years. Cora appeared to have kept everything Charlotte had drawn over the years and made a collage of them across her living room wall.

'Take a seat. Would anyone like a drink?' Cora asked.

'No, thanks,' Sarah said as she walked over to the sofa and sat down.

'I'm fine, Mum,' Jake said as he sat down next to Sarah, taking her hand in his and placing it in his lap as a sign of support.

'So, where do you want to begin?' Cora asked as she sat on the small pink beanbag next to the toy box.

'At the start,' Jake chimed in.

'Okay. Sarah, this is going to be a lot to take in, but your dad, Ben, and I went to high school together. We had an on-again, off-again secret relationship from the age of fourteen until we left high school. We kept it quiet because, as you and Jake know from experience, we knew how our classmates and even our parents would react. I mean, your family has always been wealthy, Sarah. In my family, we had to work for everything we had. So we decided to call it quits when we left school because we were going in opposite directions. He wanted to be a doctor, and I was just trying to make ends meet. I kept to myself for the next eight years and didn't date much. I then met Jake's dad. You can guess how that story went. I fell pregnant early on in our relationship. He fled as soon as he found out, and he hasn't been seen since. Ben had met your mum during that time, then she had your older brother, and then she was pregnant with you and your twin. We were all still in the same town, so even though we didn't interact, it wasn't hard to hear what was going on. When you were six years old, Ben came to visit me. We were really struggling at the time. My mum had recently died, and I couldn't afford to keep food in the cupboard. He claimed he just wanted to catch up as his son and Jake were becoming friends at school.' Cora stopped as she quickly excused herself to grab a drink from the kitchen.

Sarah felt sick to her stomach because she could see where this story was going. She hoped to hell that she and Jake didn't have a sibling in common. Maybe she was overreaching, and she wished she was, but from what she knew of her father, she wasn't. It would not surprise her in the least if he'd had an affair. He was distant, uninterested, and had far too many young pretty assistants over the years, all of whom she'd suspected were hired for reasons other than their brains. It would also explain her mum's bitterness and resentment of Jake. She took a deep breath. *One. Two. Three. Four.* as she tried to control her breathing.

'You okay?' Jake asked, squeezing her hand.

'A lot to take in already.'

Cora walked back into the room and sat back down. 'Where was I up to? Oh, yes, when Ben first came by, when you were kids. We had a few drinks, and he told me that his marriage was failing and that he was about to divorce his wife. We flirted a little, and he came by a couple of times a week to blow off steam. I was getting heavy into my drinking at the time, and he enjoyed the freedom and the party, I guess. I've made many mistakes in my life, but my biggest regret is letting the drink become more important than being a mother. After partying one night, we ended up sleeping together. Over the next few months, it became a habit for him to drop by whenever he could, and we'd have a drink and end up in bed. That is, until my drinking became even more of a problem for him. He'd show up, and I'd already be trashed. For me, days and nights became a blur. Everything became a blur, including Ben and even my own son. Ben stopped showing up, but I was usually too drunk to care. I'm not sure how I didn't have my son taken away from me, or how he grew up to be the amazing young man he is,' Cora choked out, her eyes welling up with tears as she cast a glance at Jake.

Sarah gripped Jake's hand. She'd guessed over the years that a lot of her father's business trips didn't involve any business at all, but hearing it out loud was so foreign to her. She was used to quiet denials, whispered accusations, and tightly wrapped secrets. It felt liberating to have someone tell her the truth about her father, for once.

Cora took a deep breath before continuing. 'The years after that were a blur. Looking back, I can only remember bits and pieces, the different men I was seeing and partying with, scraping enough money together to get my next drink. Jake putting me to bed a lot because I was too drunk to move. Then, when Jake was sixteen, I became very ill, my muscles stopped working properly, and I could hardly move. So I went to the doctor for the first time since I was a kid. Ben was on duty at the surgery that day, and we got talking. He wanted to help me clean myself up, or so he said at the time. We swapped numbers and started talking again. He was still with Charisse, but he told me they only stayed together for the kids. I guess I wanted someone to save me. Someone to come along and look after me, to take the burden off me. He started dropping by the house again, and we soon jumped back into bed together. This lasted about two years. He helped me stay sober, and I never expected anything from him. After an argument with Ben, I fell off the wagon and ended up at The Blue Bell, where I met Mike. He lived in the council flats not too far away. He was nice and paid attention to me when I needed it the most. He bought me drinks, one thing led to another, and he ended up coming home with me.'

'Mike! I think I ran into him the day I went to confront Jake after he dumped me via text. He was looking for you,' Sarah interrupted.

'That sounds about right,' Cora replied.

'Sorry for interrupting. You were saying?'

'Yes, so I brought Mike home with me that night. Jake wasn't home at the time, and honestly, I'm not even sure where he was. My head wasn't screwed on right at all. I wasn't thinking straight. I kicked Mike out the following day and went on with my business. A few weeks later, I missed my period and found out I was pregnant. I decided to keep the baby right then and there, that this would be my second chance at motherhood and my last chance to stay sober. I tried to keep it a secret for as long as I could, but once I started showing, I had no choice but to come clean. Jake was one of the first people I told. Then I told Ben, and he didn't take the news well at all. He walked out halfway through the conversation. I guess word got out that I was pregnant, because Mike soon showed up at my house as well. I'd completely forgotten about our night together. I was so certain that the baby was Ben's that I didn't even consider Mike. Charisse showed up at my door a few days later, and you know what happened after that. At first, there was a lot of back and forth with your mum. That is, until I agreed to the DNA test, and it was revealed that Ben was not the father. After that, she backed off, and we didn't speak again. After a couple of years down south, I wanted to come home. A lot of bad stuff happened to me here, but it's home, and I wanted to face my fears and make a better life for myself in the place I always told myself I couldn't have.'

Cora exhaled a deep sigh of relief as she finished explaining. Like telling Sarah and Jake this story was a weight off her soul.

'I don't know what to say,' Sarah said. 'That's a lot to take in.'

'I know. Take as long as you need. I'm around if you have any questions—'

They were interrupted by the sound of the kitchen back door swinging open. They all jumped to their feet and went to see who it was.

A small dark-haired girl with bright green eyes dashed towards them.

'Charlotte, you stop right there and take your shoes off, young lady,' Cora shrieked as soon as she saw her. 'All I asked you to do was take off your muddy shoes when you come into the house. Now, look at what I have to clean up.' She cast a glance over at the muddy footprints on the kitchen floor.

Charlotte laughed as she looked at her mother's face before bending down, taking off her wellies, and running towards Jake.

'JAKE!' She jumped into his arms, shrieking with delight.

'How have you been, kid?' Jake said as he drew her into a hug.

'Good, and who's this? Is it your girlfriend?' Charlotte asked cheekily, with a big grin on her face, after he put her back down.

Sarah smiled. 'I'm Sarah.'

'Hi, Sarah. I'm Charlotte, but I guess you already knew that.' She grinned as she turned to run up the stairs. 'I'm getting changed. Don't miss me too much.'

Sarah laughed. 'She's sassy, isn't she?'

'You're telling me! She's a handful, but she's a good girl.' Cora smiled.

They all spent the next hour together. Sarah got to know Charlotte, who was a hilarious little girl. She was always quick to make sarcastic comments and seemed to adore and look up to her big brother a lot. When they finally left Cora's, Jake took Sarah's hand in his.

'Well, I don't know about you, but I could use a drink after that.'

'Absolutely!'

Chapter Fifteen

THE NIGHT OUT

BRITNEY WAS FINISHING UP her eye makeup for the night ahead. She and Dylan had made plans to go out for a few drinks. Since they'd decided not to let that kiss interfere with their growing friendship, it had grown stronger than ever. Dylan had been glued to her side outside of work since she'd told him about meeting Ian, always offering to help her with the shopping or things around the house that needed looking at, playing with Noah, or simply coming over to hang out. She hadn't seen Ian and his wife since that fateful day a couple of weeks ago.

She and Dylan decided to spend some adult time together tonight. Noah had been with them every time they hung out, and they thought it would be a nice change to sit down and have a drink somewhere. Britney also didn't have much of a social life. So she was ecstatic to have a night to herself. She was wearing a new strappy black dress that fell to her knees, which she'd had her eye on for a while and was finally able to buy after saving up enough money. She was also wearing a new pair of tall black boots.

'You look amazing,' Millie, her babysitter for the night, complimented her as she sat down on the sofa.

'Thank you.' Britney smiled as she reached for her red lip gloss.

After applying her lip gloss and checking herself over in the mirror, she said, 'Okay, Noah is in bed. I'll be back around one a.m., as discussed. Thank you so much for doing this,' she added, grabbing her bag from the sofa.

'It's fine. I don't have anything else to do tonight.' Millie grinned as she reached for the TV remote.

After saying her goodbyes, Britney walked out of her flat and began her journey to The Blue Bell, where she was meeting Dylan for the first drink of the night. She was in the mood for a gin and tonic. She arrived after about fifteen minutes of walking. She hoped she didn't arrive before him; she would feel awkward just standing around on her own. Plus, it wasn't like she had anyone to even talk to, to pass the time with, as she wasn't exactly on speaking terms with a lot of people. The only time Britney was even remotely sociable was when she was at work, but that came as part of the job.

Luckily, as she passed through the pub door she noticed Dylan standing at the bar, dressed in a white T-shirt that fit nicely across his biceps, and blue jeans. She noticed his dark, messy short hair as he chatted with the bartender and wondered how someone could pull off the bedhead look so well. Then, as butterflies erupted in her stomach, she walked over to him.

She had felt the same butterflies when she'd first met Ian all those years ago, but they had vanished quickly. She'd liked Ian, and she'd even thought she loved him, but she had recently begun to second guess that.

'Hello, you!' she said softly when she got to Dylan's side.

He moved his gaze to her, giving her a quick once-over before breaking out in a small smile, 'Hey, you look gorgeous.'

'Thank you. You getting the first round in, then?' She grinned.

'Sure. What are you having?' he asked, raising his pint.

'Gin and tonic, please.'

'You heard her,' Dylan laughed and said to the bartender.

Britney cast a quick glance across the room and saw none other than Liz Beatly stride into The Blue Bell, as if she were the queen of England visiting her subjects and not just a regular mother from Baynor Green. *Give me a fucking break.* Britney rolled her eyes at how important this bitch seemed to think she was. Sometimes she wished something would knock Liz right off her pedestal and force her to get a job. Now that, Britney would love to see. She sighed and returned her gaze to Dylan.

'Hopefully, she doesn't see us.'

'What? Who?' Dylan asked, taking a quick look around.

'Liz Beatly just walked in. The last thing I need is her sticking her nose in our business,' Britney said with a sigh and a roll of the eyes.

'It's a small town and we're bound to run into her outside school at some point. So just ignore her, and hopefully, she won't come over. Oh, I didn't know they were coming here tonight,' Dylan said as he cocked his head toward the door. Britney looked over as Sarah Colling marched in, wearing black knee-high boots and an off-the-shoulder crème jumper dress. She looked stunning, as usual, with not a single hair out of place. Britney watched as a handsome man with short blond hair, bright green eyes, and a toned body—well, from what Britney could see, in his nicely fitted black shirt and blue jeans—walked in behind her.

'That's Jake,' Dylan chimed in.

Oh, so this was Jake. She didn't know him, but she had heard the rumours around town—and the salon—about him. She also knew he and Sarah had a long history. She was glad that they appeared to be resolving whatever had happened between them years ago.

Sarah smiled and strolled over as soon as she saw them both. Jake trailed close behind her.

'Well, this is a surprise. I didn't know you were in here tonight,' Sarah said as she glanced at her brother before turning to Britney. 'Nice to see you again.' She smiled.

She was relieved that Sarah was being friendly. She was worried that once Dylan told Sarah about Ian's return to town, their progress would be shattered, but it was clear that it had had no effect on Sarah's opinion in the least.

'Well, since we're all here, who wants a drink?' Dylan asks.

'Me! I've had such a mind fuck of a day, it's unbelievable. I have something to tell you later, Dylan, but I need to let it process first,' Sarah exclaimed as she let out a deep sigh. 'Oh, this is Jake. Jake, this is Britney.'

'Nice to meet you,' Jake said politely as he smiled briefly at her before returning his attention to Sarah.

They spent the first hour of the night in The Blue Bell talking about Dylan's travels and laughing amongst themselves. All talk of Ian was avoided, as was anything negative. They were all in need of a break from the toxic aspects of their lives. Until they were rudely interrupted by none other than Liz Beatly, who cleared her throat and stood at the front of their table, demanding their attention. The foursome's conversation came to a halt as they all turned to face the woman.

'Can we help you?' Jake asked in confusion.

'Sarah, why would you align yourself with someone who seduced your ex-fiancé?' Liz asked flatly.

Sarah smacked the table angrily. 'How is who I have friendships with any of your business? You know nothing about my life or Britney's life.'

'I know she seduced Ian into getting her pregnant, and lately, she appears to be seducing her son's teacher.' Liz snorted before giving Britney a death stare. Britney never fully understood Liz's distaste for her. She was used to Liz's snide remarks on the school playground, but she always tried to be civil. Unfortunately, she seemed extra bitchy tonight.

Jenny Moorfield walked up from behind Liz, deciding to join the party. *Now it all makes sense; as soon as Jenny is near, Liz's civil attitude towards me is long gone.*

'Oh, have you come to join the party as well?' Sarah scoffed in annoyance.

'Don't talk about something you know nothing about, Liz,' Dylan said.

Britney softly grabbed Dylan's arm to get his attention. 'It's all right! Let us not let them ruin our night.' She sighed.

'Ruin? That's what you and your mother are good at, isn't it? Ruining relationships?' Jenny scowled.

'Get over it. We were kids. You still have a grudge after all these years about my mum's affair with your dad? Take it up with them. Stop blaming me for your broken family.' Britney had lost her patience. She had been dealing with Liz's misplaced anger since they were children.

'I've had enough of this,' Sarah said. 'Liz, I heard your husband is having an affair with his secretary; you should ask him about that. It could explain why you're constantly left alone in your big house while he's always away on *business* trips. Jenny, I don't even know where to start with you. How about the fact that your husband dumped you for a younger woman, or that you've been throwing yourself at every man in town who will take you? Keith, for example, who, if you haven't already guessed, does not want to be with you. So, darling, take your stalking elsewhere. Now, both of you leave us alone. If you don't want me to get involved in your personal business, stay out of ALL of ours. Do you understand?' Sarah demanded.

Liz and Jenny turned bright red in the face before looking at each other and walking away from the table in silence. In response, Jake burst out laughing. Britney sat stunned as Dylan took another sip of his pint. She'd never heard anyone put those two in their place in such a way before. Sarah was a tough cookie who wasn't going to be pushed around by them.

'Well, you told them,' Jake choked out between bursts of laughter.

'If they don't want me to interfere in their business, they should mind their own.' Sarah snorted.

'Anyway, that's enough of that. Should we go somewhere else?' Dylan cut in as he jumped up from the table.

'All right, let's go!' Jake responded.

Chapter Sixteen

THE AFTERMATH

IT WAS SHORTLY AFTER midnight, and the main road, which had been bustling with town residents doing their shopping, socialising, and dining at the local restaurants throughout the day, was now quiet, cold, and deserted. That was, until four people came flying around the corner, laughing amongst themselves.

'We need to do this again soon,' Sarah said as she laughed.

The night had gone so well. Jake and Dylan hit it off right away, which Sarah would have expected given Jake's friendship with her twin, Ryker, and she certainly enjoyed getting to know Britney. She could see what had Dylan so interested in her. She was friendly, funny, and clearly adored her son, as Sarah could tell by her constant talk about him. Sarah was comforted that Dylan had finally found someone with whom he could connect.

They were about to say their goodbyes and part ways when they heard a loud shriek.

'What the hell was that?' Britney said as they turned their heads toward the sound.

'Stay behind us,' Dylan muttered quietly to Britney and Sarah as he and Jake walked towards the small side street where the noise had come from.

Sarah had a bad feeling about this. Her gut was screaming at her to turn around because what she was about to witness would not be pleasant.

'Please, let's just go home,' pleaded a small, timid voice as they approached.

Wait.

It had been a long time since Sarah had heard that voice, but she remembered how powerful it was the last time she heard it, five years ago at a funeral, screaming that it was all Dylan's fault that her sister had died.

'Anna?' Dylan choked.

When Anna turned to face him, Sarah noticed the colour drain from her brother's face. Anna Whitemort was Melissa's younger sister. She hadn't seen Anna since that day at the funeral; it had also been the last time Dylan had seen or spoken to anyone from Melissa's family, as far as she knew.

Sarah felt sick. Anna, red-faced and crying, was being dragged down the small dark street by her hair by none other than Ian. The rage erupting from him was terrifying.

'Take your hands off her right now!' Dylan stormed over to them, jaw set and teeth bared. Sarah didn't know how he was going to take this. She couldn't even imagine what was going on in his head right now. She cast a quick glance at Britney, who was frozen in shock.

Sarah went to run after Dylan before Jake stopped her. 'I'm not letting you go in there. Stay behind me, okay? I'm not going to let anything happen to you,' he said softly as she raised her head to look at him.

'Who the fuck do you think you are? Stay out of our business,' Ian snapped from a short distance away, his eyes darkening in rage as he turned to Dylan. 'Of course, you two would be here,' he scoffed as his gaze locked on Sarah and then Britney. 'Best of friends now, huh?'

'Ian, I'd say it's a pleasure, but that would be a lie. You clearly haven't improved over the years. Get your hands off her now, or we'll make you!' Sarah yelled. In response, Ian smirked at her before he gripped Anna's hair tighter in his fist and glanced back towards Britney. Sarah followed his gaze and watched as Britney's entire face turned white.

'I'm not going to tell you again! Get off her RIGHT NOW!' Dylan snarled as he reached for Anna.

Ian let go of Anna and slammed his fist into Dylan's face. Jake sprang into action and ran towards them. 'I told you to stay out of mine and MY wife's business!' Ian roared before Dylan took a swing and decked Ian right on his arse. Dylan dashed over to a sobbing Anna to check if she was all right. As Ian jumped up and rushed back towards Dylan for another swing, Jake threw him out of the way and straight onto the empty main road. Sarah ran to help Anna.

So Anna was Ian's wife. Sarah never saw that coming. That was a disaster waiting to happen; from what Sarah remembered of Anna, she was sweet and innocent, and Sarah had always liked her until that day at the funeral.

'Are you all right?' she asked Anna.

Dylan turned to look at Britney, still standing like a statue in the same spot. Sarah was taken back by her wide eyes, pale skin, and terrified expression.

Dylan was about to walk back over to her when he was tackled hard to the ground. Jake ran over and yanked Ian off Dylan, sneering, 'Leave now before this gets out of hand.'

'So, what? I'm supposed to leave just because two slags and their white knights tell me to?' Ian snarled.

That was enough for Jake. His rage overflowed, and he punched Ian in the nose, breaking it in the process. At the impact, Ian covered his face with his hands. Dylan was in the process of rushing towards him before—

'Stop! STOP! Please ... please. He's just had too much to drink, and he doesn't mean it.' Anna jumped in the middle, attempting to protect Ian and stop the fighting. Instead, Ian shoved her to the ground before rushing back toward Jake and retaliating with a punch of his own.

The heart-stopping scream that followed as Anna fell made the men immediately stop as they turned towards the sound in fear. Anna was sprawled across the pavement with a large red gash at the side of her temple from where she'd smashed her head once she hit the ground.

Ian rushed towards her, dropping to his knees by her side. He took both of her hands in his and squeezed them. 'Anna,' he said, his face contorted in fear. 'Are you all right?' He examined her wound with his hand on the side of her head. 'I'm fine,' she replied, clearly in pain. He leaned forward and pressed his lips possessively against her brow before declaring loudly, 'Let's go home.'

Anna struggled to stand and smiled weakly. Sarah rushed over to help her before Ian yelled at her, 'I've got it! leave us alone.'

'Are you sure you're all right?' Sarah asked, ignoring Ian.

'Yes, thank you.' Anna smiled briefly before Ian took her hand in his.

'Let's go now!' Ian grumbled.

'You're joking, right? We are supposed to just let her leave with him?' Dylan snapped.

'Dylan! Please leave it alone. This is what I want to do,' Anna replied softly before tightly gripping Ian's hand as they began to walk away.

'No! If something happens to you—' Sarah began as she attempted to reach out to Anna. Her mind raced. How was she supposed to let this woman leave with this monster after everything that had just happened?

'He's my husband. Just let us leave, please,' Anna begged before they both stormed off, hand in hand.

The silence that followed was deafening. In shock, they all watched Anna and Ian walk away until they were out of sight.

'Well, I wasn't expecting the night to end with a black eye,' Jake moaned.

'Britney,' Dylan murmured as he began to walk back over to her.

Oh shit, Sarah had completely forgotten about Britney for a few minutes there, with everything else going on. Sarah watched as Dylan took a step closer to Britney, who shook her head and took a step back in response. Dylan's face contorted in agony at her action.

'That fucker won't report us, will he? I don't need any more shit on my plate.' Jake panicked as he came up to her.

'Ian is too proud to go to the police. Plus, it could open the way to questions about his behaviour. The last thing Ian wants is for the word to get out that he's hurting her. It won't help his already tarnished reputation,' Sarah explained as she raised her head to look at him.

'Fuck that prick ... he's lucky Ryker wasn't with us,' Jake said in a huff. 'If Ryker had been with us tonight, Ian would have run for the hills.'

'Looks like they have a lot to talk about. Let's leave them to it,' Sarah said as she glanced back at Dylan and Britney and said, 'We are going to take off. I'll see you later, okay?'

'Yeah, bye,' Dylan responded briefly before returning his full attention to Britney.

The four of them finally split into two pairs and went their separate ways.

· • • • • • • · ·

BRITNEY WAS SHAKING AS she and Dylan walked silently back to her flat. *I gave him to you. I could take him away just as easily ...* The words Ian had cut her with the last time she saw him, before tonight, crept into her mind. She was terrified. She knew he was a complete dick, but the more she saw of him, the more she worried about her Noah. What if Ian did try to take him away? Britney came to a halt and leaned against the wall of her apartment building to catch her breath, closing her eyes as she felt vomit rise from the pit of her stomach. She couldn't live with herself if anything happened to Noah. She couldn't live without him. She often wondered how she had managed to live a life before him.

'Britney ...' Dylan leaned forward and softly took her hand in his. She gently pulled it back and drew herself up to go inside. When they arrived at her front door, she quickly unlocked it and walked inside, with him following closely behind her. She put on a fake smile, paid the babysitter, and waited for her to leave. Then she walked towards Noah's bedroom, kneeled next to him, and stroked his soft hair away from his sleeping face.

No, she would never, ever lose him.

She leaned forward, kissed him on the cheek, and exited his room, closing the door behind her. She took a deep breath and proceeded to the small living room. Dylan was already waiting for her on the sofa.

'Who's Anna?' she asked as she took a seat next to him.

'Melissa's sister,' he said quietly as he leaned forward and buried his face in his hands. 'She blames me for what happened.'

'Why would she blame you?'

'I was driving when the accident happened. When Melissa...' He choked. 'The car came out of nowhere and there was nothing I could do. I often think to myself that if I had taken a shortcut or gone down a different road. Things could have been different. She would still be alive today.'

Britney felt her heart plummet to her stomach. She couldn't imagine the pain of feeling responsible for someone's death, especially someone you loved. Even if it was an accident.

'I'm so sorry.' Britney whispered as she glanced over at him.

'I haven't seen her or anyone from that family since Melissa's funeral. I didn't even know she was married. Especially to him, of all people.'

Britney's eyes closed in agony; things had just gotten a whole lot more complicated. Anna, Ian's wife, was Dylan's sister-in-law. They could tell she was being abused based on what they saw tonight. Britney had seen many women in Anna's shoes over the years, time and time again. So she understood how difficult it was to walk away from something that they had grown used to and had been emotionally manipulated into believing was normal, no matter how toxic or dangerous it was.

The excuses: *he just drank too much; it was my own fault, I provoked him; I walked into a door.* Britney had heard it all before, from a variety of different women on the estate. She'd even overheard similar whispered conversations from some of the other mothers at school, who were always trying to put on a good front. But, growing up, she realised these issues were not limited to her area. Some places were simply more open about it, whereas others kept it hidden behind closed doors.

'He's going to come after Noah ...' Britney choked out.

'No, he won't. I won't let that happen. I promise you,' Dylan said as he snapped his head up and turned towards her.

Britney wished she could believe him, but she didn't know what to think anymore. Dylan was her rock, best friend, her—'I need time apart,' she began as tears welled up in her eyes.

'Wh—what?'

'I need to focus on Noah and prepare myself in case Ian comes for him. I ... I'm sorry. I just think we need to step away from each other for a while,' she said, closing her eyes tightly. She needed to focus her full attention on her son now that she'd discovered just how dangerous Ian was. She knew Dylan's connection to Anna would cause Ian to lash out, and she couldn't risk putting her son in harm's way if he did. Despite the fact that she felt as if her insides were being sliced in half, she needed to take a step back from Dylan.

'This is what you want?' he whispered as he stared at her, the shine in his eyes suggesting that he, too, was holding back tears.

She nodded and shifted her gaze to her small living room table. She couldn't look at him or anywhere else because she'd burst into tears, which she couldn't afford to do right now. Her body trembled, and her heart felt like it had been stabbed repeatedly, but she needed to keep going. Finally, she heard him get up from beside her. He leaned down and kissed her softly on the forehead before walking towards the door.

'Thank you for making me feel again,' he murmured as he walked out the door and shut it behind him.

· · · ● · ● · · ·

'STILL TWO SUGARS?' SARAH asked as she stood beside her kitchen counter, about to boil the kettle. Her overloaded head had been pounding ever since they returned to her apartment. She hadn't even had time to process everything she'd learned from Cora earlier today when another problem followed shortly after. Ian. Anna. The fight. Jake had panicked about Ian going to the police the full walk back to her apartment. Things were getting awkward now. Silent. They didn't know where to begin, but they both knew they had to talk.

'Yes, please,' he said as he approached her from behind.

She gave a slight nod. 'So ...'

'Maybe I should come back tomorrow. After the day you've had, it'd probably be best,' he said, turning to leave the kitchen.

'Why now?' she turned and said to his back as he came to a halt.

'What?' He turned back to face her.

'Why did you decide to return here after all these years? What took you so long to tell me the truth?' she asked, her anger rising once more. Why did it take him ten years to tell her the truth? Why did he come back? Why now?

'Life happened!' He sighed in frustration.

'So, after ten years, you've only now just decided to show back up into my life? You didn't even tell me straight away when you came back. No, you had to dip your toe in a couple of different options first before you told me anything!' Sarah snapped.

'No! It wasn't like that. I saw you again, and it cut me up inside. I forgot what that felt like. Being in your presence alone obliterates me! I came back for my mum and sister, but I knew when I saw you that there was a deeper meaning—'

'A deeper meaning. You changed your tune. Given that one of the first things you did when you returned to town was go on a date with that bartender.'

'Stop it. Nothing happened. I was lonely and wanted some company,' he admitted in desperation.

'You should have come straight to me. You should have told me years ago—'

'Don't you think I know that? I kick myself, knowing that I ever left you. You were the best thing that had ever happened to me. You gave my life meaning; you pushed me to be the best I could be. I should have fought for you more, and I will regret for the rest of my life not doing that. No woman I've dated since has come close to you. You are still the best I've ever had or will ever have—'

Sarah pressed her lips against his, cutting him off, her heart thumping. Then she drew back, bowed her head, and gazed at her feet. Her nerves were catching up with her actions, and she felt a knot in the pit of her stomach.

Jake pressed his finger beneath her chin, forcing her to raise her head and look at him. His eyes shone with emotion and intensity. He grumbled, 'I missed you.'

She closed her eyes. 'Me, too.' And she did. So much.

He exhaled sharply. 'Fuck,' he muttered.

His thumb brushed across her bottom lip. There was a warmth in his eyes that she hadn't seen in a long time. It took her back to the age of sixteen, when she had given him her virginity. She had felt so loved and safe at the time. As they stared at each other now, time seemed to stop. She felt the warmth radiating from his body. She reached up and kissed him again. Hard. This time, he wasn't taking any prisoners.

With both hands on her hips, he lifted her onto the kitchen counter. He stood between her legs, pressing so hard against her that she had to fight for air. She didn't care. Breathing was no longer a priority. She wrapped her arms around his neck and kissed him as deeply as she could. His mouth was so warm and had a faint mint taste to it. She couldn't get enough of him.

His hands ran to the bottom of her dress and broke away as he pulled it up over her head, his touch fiery hot against her skin. Her spine tingled, and the corners of his mouth curved into a smile. His hands caressed her sides before moving up to her stomach and cupping her breasts. He made a low, deep sound in his throat as he ran his thumbs over her nipples. As a result of the jolt through her veins, her head fell back.

He kissed her bare neck. They were both panting. She ran her hands over his shoulders and reached down to pull his shirt over his head as he pushed her legs wider open with his knee. Watching her face, he ran one hand from her breasts to her stomach and slowly slid down towards her—

'Oh,' she let out shakily.

In anticipation, she closed her eyes. In response to the sensation, she let out a small moan. He was doing something incredible with his hand, his fingers stroking a spot that made her shiver. As his other hand reached up and continued to knead her breast, she was on the verge of hyperventilating.

'Jake, I—'

He kissed her again, hard. It didn't take long for an ache to develop down below, and her hips rose to meet his hand movements. God, he knew exactly what to do.

The tension suddenly broke, and she cried out against his mouth, clutching him tightly as the spasms rocked her body. Her face was hot, as was the rest of her body.

When she regained her composure, she threaded her hands into his hair and kissed him fiercely. She crushed her hips against him, her heart rate skyrocketing, letting him know exactly what she wanted. She could tell by the hardness pressed between them that he felt the same way.

'God, Sarah,' he groaned against her mouth.

He didn't hesitate to reach around, cup her arse, and lift her up. She wrapped her legs around his waist and her arms around his neck, and her head bowed to ensure their lips never parted. He walked out of the kitchen, around the corner, and into the hallway, and kicked the bedroom's half-open door wider.

He threw her onto the bed, and she reached for the button on his jeans. He removed his shoes quickly, and she pushed down his pants, revealing a pair of black boxers that left little to the imagination. She yanked the boxers down in one swift motion, overcome by the desire to strip him naked. She let out a surprised squeal as he swooped down on top of her. He lowered his mouth to hers once more, expertly removing her underwear with one hand.

He ran his hands up her thighs, hips, sides, and breasts. She did the same, smoothing her hands over his shoulders, down his arms, and across his back. It was as if they were frantically trying to memorise each other's bodies.

He took one breast in his hand and fastened his mouth there, breaking away from her lips. She inhaled sharply, his tongue brushing against her nipple. She snatched a clump of his hair. Her whole body was covered in goosebumps. When he nipped her with his teeth, her hips bucked involuntarily. He grabbed the other nipple, and she couldn't take it anymore.

When her hands began to shake with need, when she simply desired him, she rasped, 'Jake, now.'

Then he looked up, his eyes gleaming with something unmistakable. He pressed his lips against hers. She massaged her tongue against his and grabbed his shoulders. He grabbed her hips, positioned himself, and thrust inside her, drawing in a sharp breath.

As she gasped into his mouth, her back arched off the bed. There was a brief period of discomfort before it disappeared. It was impossible to describe the sensation of having him completely inside of her. He moved out, then back in. She dug her nails into his back, and he began thrusting so quickly that she couldn't catch her breath. Her hips rose to keep up with the pace. She wrapped her legs around him, pushing him deeper. He pulled away from her mouth, staring down at her with a primal expression. She reached down and firmly gripped the curve of his arse with her hands.

He dug his hands into her hair and gripped it tightly. She bit his lip and kissed him passionately. He let out a growl in response. He sped up as if unable to stop himself, eliciting sounds from her that she had never heard herself make before. Sweat dripped down her spine as heat surged through her.

That familiar ache began to form, and each stroke threatened to shatter her into tiny pieces. 'Jake,' she gasped. 'Jake,' she sobbed. 'Oh, God.' Waves rocked through her as she shuddered along the length of him. She could feel them down to her toes. He thrust once more, letting out a shaky breath and shaking with his head in the crook of her neck. His breath was warm against her skin, and his muscles were tense beneath her hands.

They were both struggling to breathe. He didn't move as she trailed her hands up his back and held onto his shoulders. Her heart was still racing as she wondered what the future had in store for them.

Chapter Seventeen

FACE-OFF

SARAH WAS ON A mission. Her anger had finally gotten the best of her. When she awoke that morning and saw Jake's beautiful face peacefully sleeping beside her, her whole body erupted with rage. For many years, her parents had been preventing her from having this. It was agony, knowing that if their parents hadn't messed up, she could have had this with Jake instead of all the heartache and pain that followed. She'd never felt so enraged in her entire life. Not when Ian walked away without saying anything, and not even when Jake broke her heart. She was about to burst from the betrayal she felt.

She now stood at her parents' front door.

She couldn't understand how someone who had given her life and was supposed to love her could do something like this. Jake had offered last night to come along with her, but she needed to do this on her own. She took a deep breath and looked up at her large childhood home before banging loudly on the door.

'I'm coming. Just hold on a minute!' Sarah could hear her mum yelling from inside the house.

The front door swung open to reveal her mum dressed in a white blouse, a black knee-length skirt, and black heels.

'Did you think you could get away with this? Do you really hate me that much?' Sarah yelled.

Charisse rolled her eyes. 'What have I done now, Sarah? I don't have time for this. I have to meet Jill.'

'I had a nice little chat with someone yesterday. You know her, or at least, Dad knows her,' she began as she watched her mother's face drop dramatically. 'You know Cora Cremell!' she exclaimed.

'Get in here now!' Charisse said through her teeth as she drew Sarah inside the house, slamming the door shut behind them.

'What's the matter, Mum? Don't want the whole street knowing your business?'

'What's going on here?' A booming voice cut them off. Sarah saw her father stomping down the hallway towards them. 'I'm trying to schedule a meeting for tomorrow, and all I can hear is you two.' His left eye twitched in annoyance.

'Here he is! The great Ben Colling ... Hey, Dad, had any affairs lately? Oh, who am I kidding? Of course, you have!'

Sarah watched as his face turned red with rage. 'Now, listen here. I don't know who you've been talking to, but—'

'Cora Cremell,' Charisse cut in as she cast a glance at him. For a second, Sarah swore she saw a flash of genuine emotion in her mother's eyes. Pain. Devastation. Anger. But it was gone so fast that she wondered if she had imagined it.

'What lie has she been spouting now?' Ben rolled his eyes as he looked at his daughter.

'Lies? Don't even try to deny any of this. I know everything. Your entire relationship with Cora. Charlotte. EVERYTHING!' The fire in Sarah's veins burst out with the last word as she glanced back and forth between her parents.

'So, I had an affair, and what?' Ben asked. 'It's not like that kid is mine. Thank God—'

'What are you planning to do with this information?' Charisse interrupted her husband once more and returned her full attention to her daughter. Of course, the first thing that came to mind for her mother was their image. Sarah felt sick to her stomach. Rather than apologising or even attempting to explain or justify their actions, Charisse just went right to her reputation.

'Are you serious right now?'

'Yes. This is all in the past, so keep it there.'

'Keep it there?' Sarah's heart felt like it had been hit with a sledgehammer. *One. Two. Three. Four.* 'When Jake left, you sat with me while I sobbed. You comforted me,' she choked out. 'That was the first time in my life when I felt you truly loved me, but it was all a lie, wasn't it? You were just trying to protect your own secret.' Her heart was breaking, and the pain in her chest was tearing her apart. She'd always assumed that her mother loved her but didn't know how to express it.

She remembered crying on her mum's lap as she stroked her hair on the day Jake left. It was the first time her mother had shown her comfort, and learning it was all a ruse hurt her so much. Why was this so painful? She was aware her mother was a vicious woman, but she still loved her. Why did she love someone who had caused her so much pain? She fought like hell not to feel so broken over this but knowing her mum didn't love her dented her beating heart. Sarah wished she didn't love her, but this woman gave her life. Sarah would always love her, even if a more significant part of her now despised her. Her mother's face was drained of colour as she responded by looking down at the floor.

'Stop being so dramatic,' her father said, sounding bored. 'It happened. It's over. get over it. Now, if you don't mind. I have a meeting to get to, and your mother has a lunch meeting.'

'All of this started because of you! Cora. Jake leaving. Your constant obvious affairs. No wonder Mum is the way she is. Being married to a piece of shit like you shaped the person she has become.'

'Don't talk to me like that!' her father yelled. In a rage, his face turned bright red, and a vein on his forehead threatened to burst. 'How is what Charisse chooses to do my fault? What is it with you women, never taking accountability for yourselves? Cora chose to sleep with me in the same way your mother chose to stay with me despite knowing for years that I was looking elsewhere. Do you really think this is the first or only affair that your mother knows about? No, it's not. Your mother is smart enough to know she can't get better than me. So she's happy and content with the life she's created for herself. So don't blame me for the weakness of women.'

'You disgust me,' Sarah sneered before turning to face her mother, 'and you betrayed me. I hardly knew him,' she said, pointing to her father, 'growing up. You were there every day. Even if you were a complete bitch, you were still here, and that's what hurts the most. Not the affair, not what you did to Cora and Charlotte, but what you did to me. Why couldn't you ever love me? What did I do wrong?' She tried desperately to catch her mother's eye. She just wanted something. Some emotion from her. Something to show that a part of her did love her back.

'Get out! You're a disgrace for a daughter. Ian was right to run out on you.' Her father gave a dark chuckle. 'Oh, and you might as well know he's working at my practice. It's why he's back in town.'

'I wouldn't put it past you—'

'Oh, but it wasn't me who told him about the job opening. You can thank your mother and Jill for that.'

Sarah couldn't take any more. She was done. Despite her mother's usual treatment of her, Sarah had never cut her out of her life before. She finally realised that her mother didn't love her. There was nothing there, regardless of how much she wished she was wrong. After everything, her mother was also the reason why Ian was back in town? Sarah didn't realise she was crying until she felt a tear fall onto her lips. She needed to get out of there. She needed to leave before she completely broke down in front of both of them.

'I don't need any of you anymore. I have people in my life who truly love me.' Sarah took a deep breath.

'Like who? Cora's son, Jake?' Ben laughed. 'He's just like me. You know why he left London, right? I have a friend who knew him down there, and he had plenty to say. Do you want to know the real reason Jake came back here? It wasn't for you. It wasn't even for his drunk of a mother. It was because he had nowhere else to go.'

'Jake is none of your business.'

'Well, with having no job and being blackballed from the industry for sleeping with your boss's wife and all.'

Her heart halted. *What? Jake had an affair? Sleeping with his boss's wife?* She ran out of the house after catching a glimpse of her father's dark, humour-filled eyes.

Affair. Wife. Boss.

After everything Jake had seen his mother go through, after learning what Sarah's father had done, he went on to have an affair of his own with a married woman—the wife of his boss, no less. Someone who was paying him. Someone who trusted him. *He's just like me.* Her father's voice kept repeating itself in her head. *One. Two. Three. Four.*

Was that her future? Her mind flashed back to an image of her mother staring at the floor.

Was Jake similar to her father but better at hiding it? She would have laughed it off if someone had told her an hour ago that Jake had an affair; she knew him, and he wasn't like that. She now realised she was mistaken. Most women would tell her to let it go. He wasn't with Sarah at the time. But that wasn't the point. The point was that after witnessing how affairs could destroy families, he decided to start his own. She grabbed onto a lamppost and threw up right there in the middle of the road.

· · · · ● · ● · · ·

SARAH SAT FOR WHAT seemed like hours, staring at her TV. She had no idea what she was watching, and she wasn't even paying attention. Her thoughts were elsewhere. Jake had called her on and off throughout the day since she had left her parents' house. She hadn't answered the phone once. She knew she should have gone to the café today, but she couldn't bring herself to do so. She had at least made a quick phone call to Brooke to check in. She hadn't spoken to anyone else apart from that.

Numb. Cold. Sick.

Her thoughts were racing. She had no idea how she was going to get back out of that front door and back into the world of the living. On the sofa next to her, she felt her phone vibrate.

Jake is calling ...

She ignored the call yet again. She would have turned off her phone but she couldn't in case there was an emergency at the café and Brooke needed her. She buried her face in her hands as she heard her phone's text notification sound. She hadn't gone through her texts yet. She sat up again and reached over to check them.

Jake: How did it go?

Jake: What happened? Are you OK?

Jake: Sarah, I'm worried, please get back to me.

Jake: Why are you ignoring my calls?

Jake: If you don't pick up, I'm coming over.

No, she wasn't in any condition to see him right now.

Sarah: I know about your affair. Your boss's wife, Jake? Really? After what an affair did to our families, to us? Don't talk to me. I really don't want to see you. You're not the person I thought you were.

She slid her phone back onto the table and stared off into the distance. She had sex with this man less than twenty-four hours ago. How life could change in such a short span of time was unbelievable. The ups and downs were like a rollercoaster or the waves in the ocean.

Up. Down. Up. Down.

That was life, and she had no idea how to deal with it, but she guessed no one ever did. Everyone just trod along carefully in the world, hoping for an up and never a down. It never worked out like that, though.

She didn't know how long she had zoned out for before a loud knock broke her out of her thoughts.

'Let me in. Please, Sarah, listen to me.' Jake's pleading voice, followed by another knock, came from the other side of her apartment door. *One. Two. Three. Four.* The knocks were perfectly in sync with her counting.

Sarah remained seated on the sofa. Not making a sound. Quiet. She lacked the energy to speak, cry, or feel anything. Numb. Her entire body was paralysed.

'Sarah, please don't do this.' As he continued to knock, she noticed a tremor in his voice.

She walked to her front door and dropped her forehead against it.

'Jake ... please, I need you to leave. Please just leave me alone,' she mumbled through the door.

'I can't. I ... I love you! Don't do this. Not after everything we have been through. It can't be all for nothing. Please just let me in. Let's talk about this.' She heard the panic in his voice—the tremble and slight stutter in his words.

'That's the thing. I'm sick of talking about things. It's one thing after the other. I can't do it anymore. I won't do it. We just need to accept that we aren't right for each other. The universe keeps finding some way to tell us. I can't deal with this. I can't be with someone who can easily jump into an affair. I have been affected by enough affairs to last me a lifetime, and I will not put up with it in my own love life too.'

'Sarah, I made a mistake, but I didn't expect to see you again. I messed up. I really did, but that was before you came back into my life. You have to understand I would never, ever ... please,' he said quietly. Distraught. She could hear the pain in his voice

'Please just leave,' she said again as she finally drew away from the door and walked into her bedroom, closing her eyes, ignoring his knocking and pleading as she went.

Chapter Eighteen

GIRLS NIGHT OUT

BRITNEY'S LONG BLOND HAIR blew around her face in a tangle. She stood outside one of the local Italian restaurants, dressed in a black skater dress and black heels, waiting for Brooke and Sarah to arrive. Sarah had messaged Britney out of the blue—Britney was sure she got her number from Dylan—and asked if Britney wanted to join her and her friend Brooke for a girls' night out.

At first, she thought about declining. Regardless of how much she liked Sarah, she wondered if striking up a friendship with her would attract Ian's attention. She thought about it for a couple of days before she agreed. After dwelling on it, Britney concluded that Ian didn't seem particularly interested in Sarah or in the people she was hanging out with, based on their brief encounters.

She had begun to feel isolated and lonely since she had distanced herself from Dylan more than a week ago. Which was strange given that she had spent the majority of her life alone, but she had gotten used to having a friend. So she pushed herself to accept Sarah's invitation and join them both for a night out. Luckily enough, Millie—who babysat Noah last time—was available.

Britney heard high heels smack against the pavement while checking her phone. She glanced up and smiled when she saw Sarah approaching her. She was wearing a silky blue halter-top, a knee-length dress, and black wedges, and her hair was up in a perfect bun with small brown curls falling over her ears. Brooke was walking behind her, dressed in a nice cream jumper, blue jeans, and black boots, her long brown hair down in loose curls. The difference between the two women was evident. Despite this, they were the best of friends.

'Does it bother you how different we are?'

'No, why would it? I'm tired of my own company, so why would I want to be in the company of others just like me?' Dylan smiled.

'Britney!' Sarah's greeting jolted her out of her thoughts. She needed to stop thinking about him. She kept telling herself she was distancing herself from Dylan to concentrate on her son and keep him far away from Ian. That was one reason, but there was another, one she didn't want to admit to herself. He was getting too close too fast, and she was terrified. Then came the ultimate slap in the face: learning that Ian's wife, Anna, had been Dylan's sister-in-law. That had taken an emotional toll on them both, and she didn't know how to deal with it. She still saw Dylan when she dropped Noah off and picked him up after school, and while they exchanged awkward glances, she avoided speaking or interacting with him.

'Hey! I'm so glad you're here because I'm starving,' Britney said as her stomach growled.

'Yeah, sorry we're a few minutes late. This one here,' Brooke said before quickly glancing at Sarah and laughing, 'was having a so-called "hair crisis."'

'Shut up!' Sarah playfully scowled before turning to face the restaurant's entrance, 'Shall we go in then, girls?'

They walked into the restaurant and were quickly directed to their table. Britney was surprised that Sarah was able to get a booking so quickly, but that's what happened when you knew people; it was easier to get things done. The waiter took their drink orders and handed them menus as soon as they were seated. Britney could smell the delicious food and couldn't wait to try some of it. The restaurant was small, but it had an elegance that no other place in town possessed. Although the lighting was dim, each table had a lit candle in the centre. The walls were cream-coloured with fantastic art pieces sprayed across them, and smiling, well-dressed servers rushed around taking orders. The ideal location for a date. She wondered if Dylan—No! She needed to stop thinking about him.

'So, Britney, tell me about yourself. I don't know anything much about you, apart from the obvious,' Brooke said.

'I work as a hairdresser at Bailey's, and I guess that's it. I'm sorry, I'm not very interesting.'

'Don't worry about it. I'm not either. I work as a manager at Sarah's café, helping her run the place, and I live in a small, dusty flat, but I'm saving up to get the hell out of there and get somewhere nicer soon.'

Sarah groaned, rolling her eyes. 'I've told you. Why don't you just come and live with me? I have a perfectly nice, big two-bedroom apartment. You could move into the spare room.'

'I don't want handouts. I've told you this many times. You already gave me a big break, letting me manage the café for you.' Brooke huffed, crossing her arms across her chest.

'It's not a handout!'

'Yes, it is.'

'Drinks?' The waiter interrupted their little spat, which Britney was thankful for. She'd only recently met Sarah and didn't know Brooke, so sitting here while they had their little back and forth was awkward as hell. Nevertheless, they accepted their drinks, gave the waiter their food order, and handed back their menus.

'Well, isn't this a strange sight?' a voice interrupted as the waiter walked away.

All three women turned to look at none other than Cherry Walker, who was walking towards their table with Sarah's brother, Ryker, not far behind her. This was the first time that Britney had seen Ryker up close. He was extremely attractive in a rough sort of way, but he appeared to be the type of man who would swallow you whole and spit you out. Not Britney's cup of tea at all. Maybe five years ago, but not anymore.

'Cherry.' Sarah smiled briefly before turning to face her brother.

'Hey, sis. So, listen, word on the street is that Mr. Posh Prick is crying about having a busted nose.' He laughed. 'Why didn't you or the lads tell me about their fight with him the other night? I can't believe I missed it.'

Britney's heart dropped into her stomach. She felt sick with anxiety just hearing about that night.

'I'm glad you weren't there because the damage you would have done would have landed us all in jail,' Sarah said with a sigh and a roll of the eyes.

'No, it wouldn't have. If we had been arrested, I would have had us out in no time,' he said confidently. Even though his green eyes matched

Dylan's, they were completely different. The swagger, the confidence, even the way they spoke. Britney wouldn't have known they were related if they didn't share the same last name.

She picked up her phone when she noticed it light up next to her.

Dylan: Hi

Britney bit her lip as her heart thudded in her chest. Should she reply? One reply wouldn't hurt, right?

Britney: Hi

He read her message straight away.

Dylan: Sarah told me you were hanging out with her tonight.

Before replying, she glanced up quickly at Sarah, who was still engaged in conversation with Ryker.

Britney: Yes.

She quickly clicked her screen off and tossed her phone to the side. It was fine to make small talk. Just because she was taking a step back didn't mean she'd never interact with him again, did it? Her chest tightened at the thought.

The waiter came over to the table with their starters. Cherry wrinkled her nose as she gazed at Brooke's food.

'Are you sure you want that, Brooke?' Cherry snorted.

'What's that supposed to mean?'

'I just mean ... are you sure you should be eating any more than you already are?' Then, in disgust, she scanned Brooke from head to toe.

Brooke's face flushed as she gazed down at the table.

'That's enough. There's nothing wrong with how she looks. Move now, or you can spend the rest of the night alone,' Ryker barked.

'Why do you always defend her? What, only you can argue with her now? Why do you care about what's said about this bitch? You don't defend me or care about what anyone says about me,' Cherry whined.

'Because the vast majority of what people say about you is accurate. Now, either shut up and walk over to our table or leave and don't call me,' Ryker demanded, rolling his eyes.

Cherry immediately shut up and walked off, finally leaving them in peace. Ryker followed her.

Sarah burst out laughing. 'Well, that showed her. I can't stand her.'

'I don't know why he keeps her around,' Brooke snorted as she took a sip of her glass of wine. 'Anyway, what's going on with Jake? After that big blowout with your parents, you haven't mentioned him much.'

Britney saw the colour drain from Sarah's face and immediately knew this was a sore subject. Whatever had happened between them, Sarah wasn't ready to talk about it, which was fine with Britney. She wasn't ready to talk about Dylan either. 'So, Brooke, you seeing anyone?' she asked, hoping Brooke would take the bait and change the subject.

Brooke noticed Sarah's reaction right away and jumped at the chance to change the subject from her previous question. 'Single as a pringle. Why? Know anyone?'

'Not really. I don't get out much.' Britney laughed as she quickly glanced around the room, catching sight of Ryker and Cherry's table. She caught Ryker's eye as he looked their way and followed his gaze to Brooke. When he realised he'd been caught, he immediately returned his gaze to his date.

'So, Britney, you should bring that kid of yours to the café. We make the best pancakes.' Brooke smiled.

'He does love pancakes.' Britney laughed. 'So, do any of you know Mrs. Beckon?'

'Unfortunately,' Sarah huffed. 'She's a friend of my mum's.'

'Well, she came into the salon yesterday and began telling everyone who would listen that she had seen Cherry screaming at a woman in the middle of the supermarket earlier that day. Ryker's name was mentioned a couple of times.'

'Which woman?' Brooke jerked her head in Britney's direction.

'No idea. She didn't say.' Britney shrugged.

'Sounds like Cherry. Ryker isn't her boyfriend, and she knows it. He's told her that straight up.' Sarah rolled her eyes.

'Yeah, but who was the other woman?' Brooke asked yet again.

'It was most likely one of Ryker's flings,' Sarah responded as she sipped her wine.

'Oh,' Brooke mumbled as she looked back down at her plate.

'Has anyone seen or heard from Anna since the other night?' Sarah asked in a worried tone.

'No,' Britney responded. 'I hope she's okay, though. I feel horrible for her.'

'I saw Ian coming out of the supermarket yesterday. But he was alone,' Brooke said as she cut into her meal.

'Why do you keep looking over there?' Cherry shrieked across the restaurant.

Sarah groaned into her glass of wine. Brooke turned quickly towards the couple while Britney looked down at her food. It appeared she wasn't the only one who had noticed.

'I'm not! You know what? I've had it with you. You're not worth any of this!' Ryker stood and stormed out of the restaurant. Cherry ran after him and gave Brooke a dirty look as she passed. Britney wondered what that was all about.

· · • • · • • • ·

BRITNEY WAS TENSE. SHE considered turning around; perhaps they didn't have any available tables anyway. It was a Sunday morning, after all, but as she looked down at Noah's excited face, she knew she had to suck it up and push through her nerves. So she exhaled fully as she pushed open the door to Terrance Café. The first person she saw when she walked in was Brooke, who grinned as she looked up from her notepad at the counter.

'I thought we'd take you up on that pancake offer.' Britney's grip on Noah's hand tightened slightly as she smiled nervously.

'You're in luck. We've got a special today.' She smiled as she rushed over and knelt beside Noah. 'And who might this handsome little man be?'

'Noah!' he said, grinning. 'What's your name?'

'Hi, Noah. I'm Brooke, and I have the best pancakes for you today. Do you like chocolate?' she asked as she drew herself back up to her full height.

'I love CHOCO!' he shrieked.

'Why don't you both come with me, and I'll put you in a nice booth?' Brooke said as she led them to a corner booth by the window and handed Sarah a menu.

'Thanks. Is Sarah here today?' Britney asked as she accepted the menu.

'Yes, she's in the back. I'll go grab her. Can I get you any drinks?'

'I'll have a coffee, please, and he'll have an orange juice.' Britney cracked a grin.

She was curious how Sarah would react to Noah. He had his father's blue eyes, but they weren't as dark and cold as Ian's. Instead, Noah's were open and loving.

Brooke rushed off to get their drinks and let Sarah know they were here. This was going better than Britney had anticipated. She noticed Sarah heading towards their table with their drinks a few minutes later.

'Here you go.' She smiled as she placed their drinks in front of them. 'Aren't you a cute one?' she said to Noah.

'I'm Noah.' He grinned as he took a big gulp of his juice.

'I know. Your mummy has told me all about you. I'm Sarah.' She smiled and looked at Britney. 'He's beautiful. Those eyes ... the only thing worth getting from you know who.'

'I know. He's such a good boy, too.' Britney smiled proudly.

'I'm glad you brought him in. So, what can I get you?'

'I'll have the full breakfast and—'

'CHOCO pancakes!' Noah shrieked.

'All right, one full breakfast and some chocolate pancakes coming up.' Sarah jotted down their order on her notepad. 'I'll be back soon with your breakfast,' she added before walking off to greet another customer.

'The ladies in here are nice, Mummy.'

Brooke dashed over, clutching some crayons and a small colouring book. 'Oh, I nearly forgot. Here you go,' she said as she placed them onto the table before scurrying back off.

Noah immediately opened the book and began colouring. *Well, that should keep him occupied for the time being.*

Noah sat colouring for the next fifteen minutes while Sarah and Brooke came over every now and then to check on them. Britney was finally able to unwind, when—

'Mummy, look, it's Mr. Coll.'

Britney immediately glanced towards the door and saw Dylan walk in. She had gotten used to seeing him around the school, but they still avoided interaction whenever possible. That didn't mean the butterflies in her stomach had stopped every time he was in her presence, though.

'Oh, yes.'

'Mummy, how come Mr. Coll doesn't come to ours anymore?' Noah asked.

She didn't know how to reply to that. Luckily, she didn't have to because Brooke came rushing over with their food at that exact moment.

'Eat your pancakes,' Britney said to Noah after thanking Brooke, who returned to the kitchen to bring out another order.

'I like CHOCO pancakes,' Noah said around a mouthful of food.

'Don't talk while eating.'

Noah swallowed his first large bite after closing his mouth. 'Sorry, Mummy!' he said before leaping up in the booth and yelling, 'Mr. Coll!' at the counter where Dylan was ordering a drink.

Dylan's head jerked in their direction, and a bright smile flashed across his face as he saw Noah. He took his drink from the counter and walked over to them. Britney's entire body shivered at the sight of him. As he approached, the somersaults in her stomach increased. Finally, she drew Noah back down to his seat to finish his breakfast.

'Hello, Noah,' Dylan said, smiling.

'Hi, Mr. Coll! I have been practicing my art. Look.' He waved his colouring book.

'So you have.' Dylan shifted his gaze to her. 'Hey, Britney,' he mumbled.

'Hi,' she squeaked awkwardly.

'Anyway, I'll see you at school tomorrow, Noah.' He smiled before walking back to the counter.

Britney glanced back at Noah. 'Come on, finish your breakfast.' Her heart was in her throat as she tried to maintain a casual demeanour in front of her son.

She glanced over at the counter and saw Dylan sitting in one of the chairs overlooking the café. His eyes were locked on hers. She quickly looked down and resumed her meal. As she continued to eat and engage with Noah, she couldn't stop looking over at Dylan, as if her gaze was drawn to him. As soon as his eyes would catch hers, she would quickly glance away. She asked a nearby waitress for the bill after they had finished eating. Then she returned her gaze to Dylan, who was preparing to leave.

'Miss, your bill has already been paid,' one of the young waitresses told Britney when she signalled for the check.

'What? I haven't paid yet.'

'Oh, someone took care of it earlier for you.'

'Who?'

'Him over ...' She cast a glance at the empty seat where Dylan had been.

Britney immediately jumped up and rushed to the door to see if she could catch him and give him the money back for the food, but he was already long gone by the time she stepped outside.

Chapter Nineteen

ANNA

THE BUSINESSES ALONG THE centre of town were empty and dark, with 'closed' signs on every window. It was close to midnight on a Tuesday, so Sarah didn't expect anything less on her way home from Brooke's apartment. She walked past the Italian restaurant where she, Britney, and Brooke had dinner last week. She could hear muffled voices and loud music coming from The Blue Bell a few streets away. Thankfully, it was in the opposite direction, as she didn't want to run into anyone she knew and be forced to socialise. She was exhausted. All she wanted to do was curl up in her cosy pjs and sleep. She would be up bright and early the next day to open the café.

Jake was still attempting to contact her on a regular basis and had even stopped by the café a few times, pleading with her to listen to him and give him another chance. She ignored all his phone calls and messages, and she avoided even looking at him when he came into the café. She would completely ignore him, walk the other way, and let one of the other girls serve him.

She rolled her eyes as she heard a loud, drunken, playful scream. Didn't anyone have anything better to do on a Tuesday night? Sarah decided to take a shortcut through an alley a few streets away from her home. What she didn't expect was the loud thump that brought her to a halt. Her eyes tried to adjust to the darkness as she tried to assess the threat of danger. Suddenly, she saw the outline of a tall figure running down the other end of the alley towards the street.

She took a few deep breaths and ducked behind a small side bin—not that it would do her any favours if the individual decided to turn back—and not even a minute later, a bright light lit up the alley, almost blinding her, and she heard a car engine roar to life. She cast a glance at the person who had jumped into the driver's seat as he quickly backed away and turned the car around before disappearing into the darkness. She could spot that face from a mile away. It was one she'd been trying to avoid since he returned to town.

Ian.

Once darkness descended back down the alley, she breathed a sigh of relief and continued walking, wondering what Ian was up to. She was getting closer to the entrance when she heard a small sound that stopped her in her tracks.

Sarah looked around. She had a sinking feeling in her stomach.

A soft cry startled her. 'Help.'

She shifted her gaze to the sound and noticed the shadow of a person attempting to shuffle out from behind a black bin. As Sarah got closer, one of the streetlights flickered towards the alley, and she caught a glimpse of red hair spilling out from behind the bin.

Sarah immediately rushed over. 'Are you okay?' she asked, panicking as she struggled to pull the bin out of the way. She took out her phone and quickly turned on the torch to get some light.

What she saw shook her to the core. Anna was half-conscious, sprawled out, with red handprints on her neck and face. As she tried to sit up straight, her head rolled back and forth.

Sarah went straight to Anna's side and began slowly helping her up when she noticed blood trickling from the back of her head.

'Can you understand me?' Sarah asked. 'It's going to be okay. I'm going to call the police right now, and they should be able to help you. I will stay with you.'

'No! No police, please, I beg you,' Anna moaned as she regained her bearings.

'Why not? Look what he's done to you. He should be in jail!'

'You don't get it. Reporting him will end up being more of a problem for me than for him. You are aware of his family's status and power ...' Anna sobbed softly. Once she was on her feet, she leaned against the wall.

'Okay. Let's get you somewhere safe. You can come to my place,' Sarah mumbled as she reached over to drape Anna's arm over her shoulder in an attempt to relieve some of the strain.

As they walked towards Sarah's apartment building, she was gladder than ever that she only lived a street away. In addition, the complex had an elevator—which she usually avoided—so she wouldn't have to struggle to get them both up the stairs. Once they were inside her apartment, she helped Anna sit on the sofa.

'Can you tell me what happened?' Sarah asked as she took a seat next to her.

They sat up through the night as Anna told Sarah about her relationship with Ian. How they had first met when he moved to her town, five years ago, it was the week after her sister's funeral, and it felt good to have someone new in her life during that awful time. He had been so good to her at first, how he'd treated her with respect, how he'd charmed her and her family, how he was the perfect man. He began to show a different side of himself after she fell for him and their relationship developed.

At first, it was the name-calling and his attempting to tear her down emotionally. Then the pushing and shoving started, and before she knew it, he was beating on her whenever his anger got the best of him, which was becoming more frequent. She had tried to leave him before, but he always found a way to get her back with either sweet talk or threats.

Her parents didn't pay much attention to her anymore; they had completely broken down and never recovered after her sister had died. She had no one else to turn to because she had lost her friends over the years due to Ian's possessiveness, and now she was alone in a strange town, being Ian's emotional and physical punching bag.

Sarah told Anna all about her past relationship with Ian, as well as Ian's connection to Britney and her son Noah.

By the end of the conversation, Anna was in tears. She was exhausted, and emotionally and physically hurt. Sarah promised to help her and offered Anna the guestroom for as long as she needed until she was able to get back on her feet. She tried to convince Anna to report Ian to the police, but Anna was terrified of the outcome and possible retaliation.

· · • • • · • • · ·

SARAH SAT IN THE passenger seat of Dylan's car. Sarah called him first thing the next morning and told him everything that had happened to Anna. Dylan's history with Anna made her believe he was the best person to turn to. Granted, she was unsure whether she should involve him, especially given his history with that family. But he stopped by Sarah's the next day after work and sat down with Anna. She apologised for what she'd said at Melissa's funeral, when she'd blamed Dylan for Melissa's accident, and they quickly changed the subject after that. Dylan promised to be there to help and support her as she prepared to leave Ian.

Sarah and Dylan were on their way to Ian's now to pick up Anna's belongings. Anna was still at Sarah's apartment but after a few days of wearing Sarah's clothing, which didn't fit very well due to their drastically different body shapes, Sarah offered to go and pick up some of her stuff. Anna was still in no good state to face Ian.

'Remember, we are just going in, grabbing her stuff, and then leaving.'

'I know! I know,' Dylan said.

Sarah didn't want Dylan to get into any trouble, and she knew that if he attacked Ian on his front doorstep, things would not go well for him. Ian would be straight on the phone, attempting to get Dylan in trouble. Especially with his job as a teacher. Dylan's entire career could be jeopardised. Sarah rolled her eyes at Ian's habit of using his family connections to get his own way. However, someone like Anna, who had been emotionally and physically abused for years, was abandoned in the dirt with no one to turn to, all because she was raised differently and did not have the same connections.

Money was power, and whoever had the most of it could do whatever they want. Of course, plenty of wealthy individuals had been exposed in the news and on social media for their harmful practises and corruption over the years, but how long did it take for these people to receive the sentences they deserved? Ten, twenty years. How many innocent people's lives had to be destroyed before their voices were heard?

Unfortunately, Sarah knew, they lived in a society that judged everyone based on how much money they had and who your connections were. It boiled down to this: if two people committed the same crime, and one was from money like Ian, and the other wasn't, the working-class individual would end up in a jail cell, while the other perpetrator would get a slap on the wrist.

'We're here,' Dylan said as he cut her out of her thoughts.

They pulled up towards a big white house at the end of Eastern Street. Dylan opened his car door and started to step out of the car before Sarah stopped him, putting her hand gently on his arm.

'I should go in alone.'

'After what he did to Anna? I can't let you go in there alone,' Dylan said frantically.

'I'm not afraid of him, and you walking in there with me will only give him satisfaction,' Sarah explained. 'He'll think I'm afraid to be anywhere near him without a protector, which will make him feel powerful. He needs to know that he doesn't scare me in the slightest.'

'But—'

'I've made up my mind. Please respect it.'

In agitation, Dylan huffed and ran his fingers through his hair. 'Fine, but I'm staying right outside, and if I even hear a hint of a raised voice, I'm coming in.'

'Thank you,' Sarah said as she got out of the car.

Despite her instinct to turn around and ask Dylan to go with her after all, she walked confidently up to the front door. She needed to appear strong. She didn't want Ian to believe he had won in any way. She wanted him to understand that his intimidation tactics would never work on her. She knocked hard on the front door and took a step back.

The door swung open, and Ian stepped out, looking like a mess. Red-eyed, greasy hair, and he looked like he hadn't showered for days.

'What do YOU want?' he snapped when he caught sight of her.

'I've come for Maisy, and some of Anna's stuff,' Sarah stated confidently, despite the fact that she was screaming at herself on the inside to get away from him.

'Oh, yeah? Why couldn't she come here herself?'

'Just hand over the dog, and let me have some of her stuff, and we will be on our way.'

Ian peered over Sarah's shoulder and noticed Dylan leaning against the car, staring him down.

'I see you brought backup,' he said with a smirk in Sarah's face.

Ian called out to Dylan, 'How's Britney? She's really good, right? But, of course, you know what I mean. Just make sure you wrap it up so you don't knock her up like I did—'

'Shut the fuck up. You didn't deserve her, and you definitely don't deserve Noah,' Dylan snapped. Sarah looked over at him and saw the rage wash over him in waves. She needed to get Dylan out of there because he appeared to be about two seconds away from pummelling Ian—which she would love to see, but not if it meant jeopardising Dylan's career.

'Just give me the dog,' Sarah interrupted, hoping to refocus Ian's attention on her.

'You tell Anna that if she wants Maisy or any of her shit, she can come here and get it herself. Now get the fuck off my property,' he said through clenched teeth, returning his gaze to Dylan. 'Oh, and Noah is *my* kid. If I ever wanted him here with me, all I'd have to do is take him. So Britney should consider herself lucky that I let her keep the little shit.' He slammed the door in Sarah's face.

In a huff, she stomped back to the car.

'I swear to God, if he comes anywhere near them—' Dylan clenched his teeth as he stared at Ian's front door.

'Let's leave before you do something you'll come to regret later.'

'Fine!'

As they drove away, Sarah considered offering Anna a couple of shifts a week at the café until she found a permanent job. At the very least, it should boost her confidence and encourage her to interact with new people. However, she needed to break the news to Anna about her things and the dog, and she knew that wouldn't go down well. For the time being, she'd pick up a couple of tops, a pack of leggings, and some underwear from the supermarket on her way back.

Chapter Twenty

MELANIE

MELANIE ADAMSON WAS HAVING a cracking day. She had just won five quid on a scratch card, got her dole money, and was on her way to The Blue Bell for a couple of vodkas. Things were going great for her recently. She'd been dating her boyfriend, Joey, for two months, which seemed like a long time in her book. Things were serious, and she was happy.

She took a shortcut a few streets away from her grandson's primary school. She knew all about his life, even though the rest of the town, including her own daughter, would never have guessed. So she kept her ears open and soaked in whatever she could about them both.

She was startled to hear a young boy crying. She came to a halt, turned, and walked in the direction of the noise.

'Just get in the fucking car, you little shit!' yelled a harsh adult voice.

Melanie noticed a silver car—she couldn't tell what make or model it was because she'd never owned a car in her life—with two figures standing next to it. One adult and one small child. She took a step towards them.

'NO! Where is my mummy?' a small voice screamed. Melanie dashed towards them. *What if a kid is getting kidnapped?* Melanie had seen a lot of unfortunate things in her life, but she refused to stand by and watch while some sick bastard messed with some poor kid.

'Don't start with me, kid. Get in the car NOW! Before I throw you into it!' the man warned. Melanie finally recognised the man's face: Ian Hennering. She'd heard through the grapevine that he'd returned to town. She looked down at the small figure next to him.

Noah.

'What's going on here?' she yelled angrily as she ran to them.

'Mind your business,' Ian said, not even turning to look in her direction.

'Nah, I don't think I will. Not when you're trying to shove my grandson into your shitty car, you prick,' Melanie exploded in rage.

Ian and Noah both turned to face her.

'Well, if it isn't the town bike, Melanie Adamson! Fuck off,' Ian growled before reaching down and grabbing hold of Noah's hood, pushing him towards the open car door.

'Get your hands off him now, ya bastard!' Melanie yelled as she reached over to free Noah from Ian's grasp.

'GET OFF ME!' Ian roared before shoving her roughly to the ground.

Melanie was not the type to put up with abuse from anyone. Her rage erupted. She leapt to her feet and punched him square in the face, in his already bruised nose. As blood began to pour out of his nose, he let go of Noah's arm and put his hands on his face.

'WHAT THE FUCK? YOU BITCH!'

'Come with me! Let's go!' Melanie extended her hand quickly to Noah, who promptly grabbed it. She took a turn with him and began to run.

'Get back here NOW!' Ian yelled, still holding his nose in his hands.

Melanie and Noah both ran a couple of streets until they were sure he wasn't following them. Luckily, The Blue Bell was just up the road from where they were.

'Wait, Melanie, are you all right?' A friendly voice hollered from across the street. Melanie turned her attention to the voice and noticed Sam Crucker, one of the new officers at Baynor Green Police Station. Melanie couldn't stand the scumbags at the station; she knew most of them were twisted and she didn't trust any of them as far as she could throw them. She met Sam at the station last week, when she was arrested for drunken disorderly conduct, which she thought was a fucking joke. It's not her fault that wankers approached her after she drank. Sam, from what she could tell, appeared to be one of the good guys, young, extremely attractive, and didn't look down on her. Still, she wasn't about to let him or any of those fucks know her business.

'Yeah, all good!' She yelled back as she dashed towards the pub, Noah's small hand still in hers, and ran inside. It was just after twelve p.m. on a Tuesday, so she hoped it wouldn't be too crowded and that it would just be a couple of the regulars she knew.

'Melanie. The usual? And what's the story with the little guy you've got with you today?' one of the bartenders shouted once he saw her enter. Luckily, it was a quiet day, no waiting around for refills.

'Make it a double. I had a stressful morning. Do you have a phone I can borrow? I ran out of credit.' She lifted Noah to sit on one of the barstools next to her usual spot. He hadn't said anything since they'd both run from Ian. She knew it was most likely the shock of all the fuckery, plus they had never met before. He went from one creepy bastard trying to shove him in a car to another stranger bringing him to a pub.

'Be quick!' The bartender handed Melanie his phone, and she dialled Bailey's Salon. Britney, she hoped, was still at work.

'Good afternoon, Bailey's, how can I help?' a chipper voice answered on the other end.

'Is Britney there?' Melanie asked as she accepted the bartender's double vodka and Coke and slapped a fiver on the counter.

'She's just with a client. Can I ask who's calling?'

'I'm her mum. Let her know that I have Noah here with me right now at The Blue Bell,' Melanie replied as she took another swig of her drink.

'Oh, okay, I'll let her know.'

'Great, bye!' Melanie handed the phone back to the bartender and turned to Noah. 'Your mum should be here soon. What do you want? Coke? Lemonade?' she asked.

'Coke, please,' Noah murmured, still shaken by the situation he had found himself in earlier.

'Get the kid a Coke!'

'Are you really my mummy's mummy?'

'Yah, I am. So why don't you tell me what happened today and how you ended up with Ian before I found ya?' Melanie asked as she placed a small glass of Coke in front of him.

·•·•●·●·•·

BRITNEY STORMED INTO THE Blue Bell. She had been frantic with worry ever since she received her mother's message at work. She'd immediately left work and made her way here. *Why was Noah with her?*

She panicked. *What's happened?* She looked around the pub desperately until she spotted them both and ran towards them.

'Mummy!'

'Are you all right? What happened?' she asked, squeezing Noah into a bear hug and kissing the top of his head.

'He's fine. I got there before that dickhead could do any damage,' Melanie interrupted.

Britney turned to her mum. 'What happened?'

'I was on my way here when I caught that prick shoving Noah into his car a couple of streets away from the school. So, long story short, I punched him in the face, brought Noah here, and called you,' she explained as she raised her glass to the bartender, signalling for another drink.

'What? How did he get him out of school? He's not on the approved pickup list.' Had Ian's connections gotten so far that he could now override the school's legal obligation to protect the children in their care? They had a system in place and a list of people who could pick up Noah from school, and Ian was not on it.

She wondered if Dylan knew about this. He had to have noticed Noah being taken out of school. After all, he was his teacher.

'Well, the kid told me that some Mrs. Atkin came to his class and told him that his parent needed to see him right away. Apparently, his teacher, "Mr. Coll," wasn't in this afternoon. One of the younger teachers was in charge of Noah's class for the day. The younger teacher, whoever she is, asked if everything was all right, and that Atkin bitch told her it was nothing to worry about. The bitch then took him to reception, where Dickhead was waiting for him. Noah freaked and asked where his mummy was, and Ian told him that he would take him to ya. So he took him out of the school and to his shitty car. When Noah realised you were nowhere to be found, he began screaming. That's when I stepped in, and here we are.' Melanie drank her refilled vodka.

'They took him out of class and gave him to Ian?' Britney exploded in rage. This was a place she entrusted her child to every day, and they couldn't even ensure his safety. She was furious. How could she possibly send him back there now? She needed to call the police and report Ian for attempted kidnapping, and the school required a severe investigation.

'Looks like it,' Melanie replied as she slammed her empty glass back down on the bar.

'Thank you for getting involved like you did ... God knows where Noah would be right now if you weren't there.' Britney sighed in gratitude as Noah wrapped his arms around her waist.

'I wasn't going to let the boy be kidnapped, was I?'

'No, you weren't. Come on, Noah, let's go,' Britney said as she reached down to take his small hand in hers.

'Maybe we could grab a drink sometime ... if ya want?' Melanie asked, softly tapping her fingers on the bar, waiting for a response.

'I'll let you know,' Britney replied, not knowing what else to say. Her mum had done a great thing for her today by protecting her son, but she wasn't sure if she could move on from the pain of the past. Time would tell.

'Well, you know where to find me,' Melanie grumbled as she returned her attention to the bar. 'Another one when you're ready!'

Britney and Noah made their way to the front door. Maybe she'd have a future relationship with her mum; perhaps she wouldn't. She would need to seriously consider all aspects, but first things first. She needed to sort out today's mess once and for all.

· · • • · • • · ·

BRITNEY HAD BEEN ON the phone with the police all day. Unfortunately, she felt utterly fobbed off and let down. The first person she was transferred to said they couldn't help her because Ian was Noah's biological father and didn't actually take him out of town. The second person she spoke with said she could leave a report. She repeatedly asked to be transferred to different officers in the police force, but the more she called, the less helpful they became.

She knew deep down that they were hesitant to help her because they didn't want to piss off the Hennerings, who had helped fund their newly built station. Noah was shaken, so she spent the entire afternoon with him, watching movies and playing with his Legos. She had just finished putting him to bed when she heard a knock on her front door.

Britney had called Sarah immediately after she left The Blue Bell. Sarah had offered to drop by after her shift. Britney had to warn her and Anna about Ian's instability. What else was he capable of if he could lose his mind that much by attempting to kidnap her son from his school? Furthermore, those two were at the top of his shit list.

She opened her front door, expecting to find Sarah, only it wasn't Sarah. She let out a small gasp before she quickly pulled herself together. The silence pounded as she looked up at him from under her eyelashes. She couldn't speak, couldn't move. This was the first time she had been this close to him since they'd decided to step away from each other.

'Sarah told me what happened, and I had to see you.'

Dylan looked exhausted. His dark eyes were devoid of the life she had taken a shine to. She flashed back to the first time she met him. The cold blank stare and lack of emotion had returned, and it was stronger than ever.

'Come in,' she said as she took a step back and let him in before closing the door behind him.

'I wasn't there this afternoon. If I had been, you know I wouldn't have ...' The first flicker of emotion passed through his blue-green eyes as he looked at her, and they softened. She could see his inner turmoil as he struggled to keep his emotions in check to keep that wall up.

'I know. I know.' They were like magnets; apart, they were useless, but a force pulled both of their missing pieces together to form one whole when they were close.

He gently pushed the tiny strands of hair that had fallen out of her ponytail behind her ear. 'How is he doing?'

'I've just put him to bed. He's had a long day. He's confused and has a lot of questions. Did you know it was my mum who put a stop to it?'

'Really?' he asked, his face flushed with surprise.

'Yeah, she came across them on her way to the pub and stopped it. Out of everyone, my mum was the one who saved him. I still can't believe it.' She looked down at the ground. How were you supposed to explain to your five-year-old son that his father is an abusive piece of shit who tried to kidnap him? And that he'd done it not out of desperation or love, but out of a desire to hurt her because of her friendship with his ex-fiancée, who had taken in his wife after he'd had left her black and blue in an alley?

Her face crumpled as she closed her eyes. She couldn't see Dylan, but she could hear him take a deep breath and pull her into his arms. *Weak. Useless.* As the tears streamed down her cheeks, she realised she'd reached her breaking point.

Noah. Her mum. Ian. Sarah. Dylan. Her father, whom she had never even met. Hell, even Anna. Everything that had ever happened to her came crashing down on her, suffocating her.

'Shhh, it's okay ... it's okay ...please.' The tenderness in his tone helped to calm her down as she drew back slightly.

'Your shirt,' she choked, seeing the wet patch where she had cried into his shirt. She slowly shifted her gaze back to his and was overcome with warmth. The spark of life that was absent when she'd first opened the door was back. The tenderness in his gaze made her want to weep all over again, but for a different reason.

'It's fine,' he said, reaching up to gently wipe the wetness under her eye. 'Once I heard about what happened, I called the school board and told them everything. I knew you'd be terrified to send Noah back after today.'

'I assumed it was the police who told them,' she said as she moved back, walked into the front room, and dropped down onto the sofa. He sat with her. 'They called me a few hours ago and told me that Mrs. Atkin and the others involved will be dealt with. They promised me that the scum involved would never set foot on the school grounds again and that every precaution would be taken to make sure that this never happens again, but how can I believe that?'

'I'll be there, and I can promise you that with me around, nothing will happen to him. Britney! I won't ever let anything happen to that little boy.'

'I know! Where were you?' she asked as she cradled her head in her hands.

She knew she had no right to ask him, but she needed to know.

'My mum. She overdosed on prescription pills this morning. I got the phone call around ten a.m. I was the only person they had thought to call. One of the women who cleans the house a few times a week found her passed out on the bathroom floor, surrounded by pill bottles.'

Her eyes welled up with tears as she saw the emotion on his face. Her chest ached from the devastation, anger, and pain she saw. 'I'm so sorry!'

'She's okay. When she finally came to, she broke down. She hates her life, her husband, and, more importantly, the person she has become over the years. She found out that my dad was having another affair, and it just shattered her. She'd bottled up her rage for so long that she took it out on those around her, becoming a bitter and twisted shell of the person she used to be.'

She leaned in and rested her head on his shoulder. He wrapped his arms around her, and they sat in silence. Her body was pressed against his, her hand resting on his chest. He moved his hand from his side to rest softly on top of hers. Britney smiled as she looked up at him, entwined their fingers, and slowly closed her eyes, letting all the pain of today fade away.

They both needed this. *Connection. Comfort.* She didn't know how long they sat there like that until he gently pulled away from her, kissed her on the forehead, and walked out in silence. She remained glued to the sofa for a few more minutes before standing up and closing the front door behind him.

Chapter Twenty-One

RISKS

THE LAST WEEK OR so had been such a head fuck, especially when it came to Sarah's family. Dylan told her about their mother, but Sarah was still adamant that she wanted nothing to do with her. She refused to be drawn back into her parents' mess. She'd done enough running around for her mother over the years. Her parents had set their path, so now they could walk it without her. However, she still couldn't stop thinking about Jake. She'd tried everything she could to get him out of her head, but she kept seeing him again in every tall blond guy she encountered.

Why wouldn't he leave her mind or her heart? On the plus side, Anna was finally coming out of her shell, and Sarah hadn't heard a peep from Ian since Britney told her about his attempting to kidnap Noah. If Ian knew what was good for him, he ran for the hills after that incident. Anna was currently working a shift at the café with Brooke. She began working there last week, just a couple of shifts a week before she found something more permanent.

'WHERE is he?' Jill Hennering yelled as she came flying through Sarah's front door. Sarah jumped up from the sofa in fright before a shadow of annoyance took over her face when she recognised her intruder. She hadn't spoken to Jill in years, ever since Ian had walked out on her, and now she was rudely barging into her home.

'Okay, first of all, don't just barge into my home as if you have any right to do so!' Sarah snapped at Jill, who was now standing in her hallway. 'And second, where is who?'

'Don't play dumb with me. I know you know where he is!'

'Get out of my house NOW! Before I throw you out!' How dare this bitch just show up at her home shouting her mouth off? Sarah was relieved that Anna wasn't here. She couldn't imagine how that would have gone down.

'Not until you tell me what you did to him!'

'If you're talking about Ian, I haven't seen that prick in weeks.' Sarah frowned. She shouldn't have to explain herself to the likes of Jill.

'You'd better be telling me the truth. He's missing, and if I find out that you or that bitch of a wife of his has anything to do with it—'

'You'll what? Nag me to death?' Sarah cut her off, snorting at her threats.

'Don't mess with me, little girl!'

Only Jill would refer to a twenty-eight-year-old woman as a 'little girl.' Sarah didn't have time for this. If Ian had left town, then good riddance. At the very least, Anna wouldn't have to worry about running into him. As Sarah opened her mouth to reply, Jill spun on her heel and stormed out the front door.

What a bitch, Sarah thought as she locked the door behind her. She wasn't in the mood for any more unwelcome visitors. She just wanted some time to herself to sort all her cleaning and washing out before she had to get to work and start her shift. She hadn't had time to herself in a while, but of course, Jill had to come and ruin it.

She took her phone from her pocket and opened the group chat she'd set up a few days before with Britney, Anna, Brooke, and herself.

Sarah: So, guess who just stormed into my house?

Anna: Who? Tell me it wasn't Ian.

Britney: ???

Sarah: Jill Hennering. She shows up, barging into my apartment. Demanding to know where Ian is. Like I have any idea where that creep is or even want to, for that matter.

Anna: WTF?

Brooke: Why would she think you know where he is?

Sarah: Fuck if I know.

Brooke: I'm surprised that bitch didn't try to blame Ryker, as everyone in this town does when something bad happens. Not like she'd ever confront him about it, though.

Sarah: I hear you.

Britney: Ian couldn't take the heat and skipped town again. I'm calling it right now.

Anna: I agree, Britney.

Sarah put her phone back down and started getting ready for her shift. Hopefully, she wouldn't bump into Jill again today.

· • • • • • • • ·

'IF YOU JUMP ON section two, I'll cover the counter,' Sarah said to Brooke as she hurriedly took the next customer's order.

'Sure.' Brooke dashed over to section two. Becky was exhausted and in need of assistance. But it was the lunch rush, so the fact that it was so crowded was unsurprising. Sarah had been running around like a headless chicken since she'd arrived, and she hadn't given her run-in with Jill much more thought due to how busy it was.

'I'll have a latte,' Crystal Shavis, next in line, ordered.

'Sure.' Sarah got right on it.

'Jake, I haven't seen you since The Blue Bell. How are you?'

Sarah, who had her back turned, came to a halt due to Crystal's words. *One. Two. Three. Four.* 'Here you go. £2.50, please,' she said as she turned back to face them and placed the drink on the counter.

'Here you go, dear,' Crystal said before scurrying off.

Sarah knew he was next in line, but she didn't look up. She couldn't see his face right now. She wasn't ready.

'Sarah, please, just listen—' he began, his voice trembling with desperation.

'Would you please take this customer's order, Brooke?' Sarah said as she turned to serve someone else, ignoring him.

Brooke gave her a sympathetic smile before sprinting over to Jake. 'What can I get you?' she asked.

'Brooke, I need to talk to her—'

'She doesn't want to talk to you right now. So either buy something or leave.'

Sarah felt sick. She hated all of this. 'Brooke, I'm just going to take a quick break,' she said as she dashed off into the back room, hoping he'd be gone by the time she returned.

· · • • • • • • · ·

JILL HENNERING WAS A nuisance. Everywhere Sarah turned, the woman was there with a face like a smacked arse. If dirty looks and snide remarks had the potential to kill you, then she would have died at least a hundred times this week. She didn't understand why the woman just didn't get it through her thick skull that Sarah had no idea where her son was. No amount of stalking would change that. As if that wasn't enough, Jill had even gone so far as to drag Anna to one side and demand answers from her as well.

Sarah was surprised that word of Ian's disappearance had not yet spread throughout the town. On the other hand, Jill was trying to keep the situation under wraps in case he did show up and she looked like a fool. Jill hadn't shown up at the one person's door that Sarah expected her to: Britney. Sarah guessed it was because of Noah and all the questions he'd raise.

Dylan was helping Sarah and Anna move some new furniture into Anna's new room. He'd been so quiet and withdrawn lately, a change from how he'd been over the last few months. Sarah was finally getting used to having her brother back when he'd shut down again not too long ago. She suspected it had something to do with Britney. Something had happened, but she didn't want to put either of them on the spot by asking.

Britney had started coming into the café a fair bit recently, often accompanied by her son, who was such a cute little boy. Ever since Sarah had formed the group chat a bit back, all the girls had been bonding and getting to know each other better. Britney had shown up at the café a couple of times when Dylan was there, and the longing in his eyes was evident for anyone to see.

'Where do you want this?' Dylan asked, jolting her out of her daze.

'Oh, just put it over there for the time being.'

'I've been meaning to tell you. Jake Cremell asked after you when I bumped into him at the shop yesterday,' he said casually as he moved one of the large boxes across the room.

Except for the girls, she hadn't told anyone about her recent drama with Jake. She didn't feel compelled to share details about her personal life. She'd had enough of that over the years. 'Oh.'

'Oh? What's going on now? I thought you two were good.'

'It's none of your business. I don't interfere in whatever is going on with you and Britney,' Sarah snapped.

His eyes grew cold. 'Don't get snappy. I was just asking. I won't ask again.'

'Good, don't, or I'll start asking about your personal life.'

'Enough!' Anna snapped. In disbelief, Sarah's and Dylan's heads swung towards her. This was the first time they'd ever heard this woman raise her voice.

'What?' Sarah responded.

'This constant need to hurt yourselves! I've had enough of it.' She shifted her gaze back and forth between them before settling on Sarah. 'Sarah, in the short time I've known you, it's been so obvious that you're still in love with your ex, Jake, and with the way he's been coming to the café nearly every day just to catch a glimpse of you and the pain in his eyes when you pretend he's not even there, I can tell he still loves you too. I know you're hurting and that your parents have messed up your perception of love, but take it from me. Never, ever throw away someone who loves you and treats you well. Your parents are not the centre of your relationship. Stop letting their mistakes cloud your judgment. And you,' she said, her gaze shifting to Dylan. 'Melissa loved you, and you loved her, but she's gone and has been for the past five years. You can't keep torturing yourself over what happened. It wasn't your fault. I am so sorry that I ever blamed you. I was wrong and hurting. She was my sister.'

She blew out a breath and continued. 'I know you love Britney. I hardly know her, but it's clear from the way you act when her name is mentioned and the longing in your eyes when she walks into the café. However, for some reason, you refuse to accept what your heart wants.'

The silence that descended upon the room was deafening. Sarah knew Anna was right. She did love Jake and had been holding back, afraid of becoming like her mother, but did she want to give up her chance at real love because of fear?

She glanced over at Dylan and felt sick at the sight. He was as white as a sheet, and the severe pain and conflict in his eyes made her want to sob.

'But Melissa—' Dylan started, and swallowed hard.

'Is gone and would want you to be happy. She loved you so much. She wouldn't want you to spend the rest of your life alone.' Anna gave him a sad smile.

He fell back onto the sofa, his head in his hands. 'You're right. I need to go. I need some time to think.' His voice cracked before he slowly rose and walked out the door without saying goodbye.

Anna glanced back at Sarah. 'What about you? Are you going to continue to allow your parents to intervene with your happiness?'

'It's not as simple as that.'

'Jake made a mistake. He had an affair and yes, it was a shitty thing to do, but Sarah, that was before he walked back into your life. What happened led him back to you. They say everything happens for a reason. I'm not condoning what he did. I don't know that story, and neither do you. But it had nothing to do with you. It shouldn't affect your future. He loves you.' Anna sighed. 'I'll give you some space to think about what you truly want.' She jumped up and went into the spare room she had been occupying.

Sarah sat and dwelled on her thoughts. Anna was right, but where did she go from there?

· · • • • • • • · ·

SARAH HAD NEVER BEEN to Jake's new place. Things had moved so quickly that she hadn't even had time to look at the house he was renting: an isolated, small, freshly painted white bungalow on a street with only two other houses. Although the house was small, the land surrounding it was vast. It was a huge improvement over the home he had as a child.

Her heart was in her throat as she stood on his doorstep, waiting for him to answer. Her thoughts were racing. She had no idea what to say. On the way here, she had prepared an entire speech. That was thrown out the window the moment she knocked on the front door.

Jake swung open the front door, his blond hair damp and mouth-watering against his flawless skin, dressed in black sweatpants and a white T-shirt. She stood there for a moment, swooning at the sight.

'What are you doing here? Are you okay?' he asked, a worried expression plastered across his gorgeous face.

She pushed him inside by pressing her palm against his chest, kicked the door shut behind her, and smashed her mouth against his. He let out a small gasp of surprise before fisting her hair, pulling her closer, and kissing her passionately back. She let out a soft moan as she drew back.

'Not that I'm complaining, but what was that for?'

She reached up and cupped his face in her palms. 'When you left, it broke me. I became an empty shell, dragged from pillar to post by my parents and allowing them to do so because I no longer felt anything. When you left, you took a piece of me with you. I tried so hard to forget you. I got engaged and that didn't help. I hated it. Hated that I could never get over you, no matter what I did. I hadn't seen you for ten years, and yet when you walked back into my life, you returned the missing piece of me that you stole all those years ago. I got scared. When I heard about your affair—from my father, of all people—my parents' relationship flashed before my eyes, and I thought that was my future. Until someone reminded me that we are not them. I want to try again, to be with you. I love you so much. I never stopped.' Her eyes welled up, her heart in her throat. She was finally doing it. Finally allowing herself to go after what she wanted. Finally breaking free.

His entire face lit up as the happy grin that splattered across it shone. He drew her in closer as he wrapped his arms around her waist and nestled his head in her neck. 'I love you too, so much. I'll tell you everything you want to know about London, about what happened there. Every. Little. Thing. You need to trust me. I can't lose you again. I've never loved anyone the way I love you. You're it for me and always have been.' He grabbed the back of her neck and pulled her into a heated kiss.

She took a step back. 'We have a lot to talk through to make this work. No more secrets. I want to know everything.'

'Okay, I guess I'll start from when I moved down south,' he said.

Jake went into great detail about his life in London as they sat and talked about everything. How after he had finished his studies at university. He began his career in a bank and worked his way up to management. He became close to one of his co-workers, who turned out to be the big boss's wife. She began to open up to him about her unhappy marriage, her husband's constant affairs, and how he didn't want children. Jake became her shoulder to cry on until one night when things went too far between them and they slept together. He realised immediately that he had made a mistake and informed her that he was stepping back from their friendship. She had already grown fond of Jake and wanted to leave her husband for him. Jake cared for her, but not enough to jeopardise his entire career. That's what he told her. After feeling rejected one night, she ended up telling her husband anyway. Jake was fired from the company right away. For some reason, he knew he needed to get his life back on track, but the only place he could think of returning to was Baynor Green.

Honestly, this story wasn't really something Sarah wanted to think about ever again; she was just glad it was all out in the open. She was also relieved that the dark cloud that had been looming over them had finally lifted, allowing them to start planning their future together.

Chapter Twenty-Two

I LOVE YOU

BRITNEY WAS EXHAUSTED, AND she looked it. As she wiped away some of the makeup smudges from under her eyes, she let out a small groan. It had been a hectic day. In addition to being rushed off her feet, she had to deal with two complaints: the new receptionist had double-booked a one o'clock appointment, and Crystal Shavis was due in soon. That woman always had something to say. But unfortunately, she lacked all tact and used her age as an excuse.

If Britney had to hear another, *"You can't say anything anymore. People get so easily offended. They would have never survived back in my day,"* or *"No wonder she can't keep a man; a woman should always pride herself on her appearance; no one wants to marry an ogre,"* she was going to scream. If the woman wasn't insulting everyone she came across, she was gossiping about others in town.

'Good afternoon, everyone,' yelled a loud voice across the salon. *Speak of the devil.*

'Afternoon, Mrs. Shavis. The usual?' Britney asked.

'Please, dear,' She walked over to Britney, pausing to toss her large bag at one of the receptionists, saying, 'Won't you put that somewhere safe like you usually do?'

'Please take a seat here for me while I sort through the mixes,' Britney said as she walked into the back.

She quickly mixed the usual colours and walked back out to find Crystal already flipping through her usual magazines.

'How have you been?' Britney asked as she began to work on her hair.

'Very well, thank you. So I saw Ryker Colling on the way here with a group of other shady-looking men. They seemed to be up to no good. I'll never understand how everything he does just flies under the police's radar.' She huffed.

'Well, you don't know what he does, so you're just assuming at this point.'

'It's obvious to everybody in this town that he dabbles in illegal dealings!' she ranted.

Britney fell silent, knowing that Crystal had a valid point there, but she wasn't going to tell her that.

'So, is it true that you're *friends* with his older brother, Dylan?' Crystal probed nosily, interrupting the silence. Britney wasn't surprised by the question; she had been expecting it. Especially after her night out with him, Sarah, and Jake. She knew word would have caught up to Crystal eventually. She was only surprised about how long she'd held out on asking it.

'Well,' Britney responded awkwardly, not knowing what to say. 'Would you like to darken it slightly today?' she asked as she attempted to change the subject. If she were in public, she would have told her to mind her own business, but this was her place of business, and she couldn't afford to lose a client.

'No, the usual would be fine. If you are *friends* with him, then good for you. If you can snag a man of higher value than yourself, then you're doing something right,' she said matter-of-factly.

Britney had the urge to hit her over the head with the hairbrush but stopped herself. Crystal Shavis came in once a month, and Britney had grown used to her sharp tongue.

Crystal must have noticed a slight shift in her mood. 'Don't be offended, dear. Anyway, how are you and your son doing? With your son's father showing back up in town and all,' she added by way of changing the subject. Unfortunately, it wasn't as if this one was any better.

'My son is very happy, and as for Ian showing back up, that doesn't have any effect on us.'

'I saw him a few weeks ago with his new redheaded wife. Timid little thing, isn't she? Trailing behind him like a lost puppy,' she scoffed. 'Funnily enough, I haven't seen him since. I heard he abandoned his wife and ran off with someone new who caught his eye. Didn't take him long, did it?'

'You're talking about a woman whom you know nothing about. You have no idea what she's going through or what happened between them in private.'

'And you do? I didn't know you knew the new wife so well. That is very strange, indeed.'

'I think you should give Anna the benefit of the doubt before you start throwing stones at her. Anyway, I'm going to leave this on for a minute, and I'll be right back,' Britney said, and she walked away before she completely lost it.

After some small talk with her co-workers and a little back-room cleaning, it was time to check Crystal's hair to see if it was ready to wash out.

'Looks like you're ready to wash! If you want to follow me,' Britney said as she escorted her to the sinks.

'So, are you still friends with Sarah? I was shocked when I found out you were seen in The Blue Bell together,' she mumbled as Britney began washing her hair.

'Do you want to use your regular conditioner?' Britney asked in response.

They spent the rest of their time together with awkward small talk and silence. The rest of Britney's shift went fast, due to how busy it was and the fact she had to leave at three to pick Noah up from school. Luckily, the school was only around the corner.

········

BRITNEY WAS STOOD OUTSIDE the school building, shivering. Even though she was wrapped up in a crème winter coat, it was a bitterly cold day, the ground was icing over, and Britney couldn't feel her hands; she regretted not putting on gloves that morning. She could hear Jenny and Liz arguing not far away. She sighed heavily. She never understood their relationship. They were best friends one week and sworn enemies the next.

'Well, that's not what Cherry said!' Jenny snarled at Liz, raising her voice.

'Cherry is a liar! And it's not my fault that Keith dumped you!'

'According to Cherry, it is your fault. You were whispering bullshit into his ear.'

'Why would I try to ruin what you had going on with Keith? I would have to care about the two of you together to attempt that, and believe me, I have better things to do with my time.'

Britney rolled her eyes at the ridiculous display. It was as if they had never grown up or left school. They had children themselves now, but they still had catfights over the most ridiculous shit. Britney didn't know Keith well, but it was obvious he just wasn't into Jenny, from what she could tell. She needed to stop blaming others and get on with her life. On the other hand, Liz lived for drama, so it wouldn't surprise Britney if she were talking shit to him behind Jenny's back.

'And anyway, why would you believe Cherry when she is pathetically running around after Ryker, who clearly does not want her arse?' Liz snorted.

Britney was relieved that the conversation was cut short when the school doors flew open and the students poured out. Noah was at the front, a big grin on his face.

'Mummy!' he yelled as he dashed over to her and threw himself at her.

'Good day?'

'Yes! Asbelle and Freddie are friends again,' he exclaimed, slightly lisping as his excitement bubbled up.

'That's great!' Britney said as she took his hand in hers and began to walk out of the playground, but then she noticed Dylan standing at the front of the school, looking at her with a soft smile on his face. Her heartbeat sped up. Something was different about him today. His expression appeared to be lighter in some ways. It was as if a huge weight had been lifted off his shoulders.

Noah smiled as they passed Liz and her daughter, Isabelle. 'See you tomorrow, Asbelle.'

She responded with a giggle before reaching over and giving him a small hug. It was cute, but her mum didn't seem impressed.

'Let's go, Isabelle,' she said as she pulled her daughter away.

'Bye, Asbelle.' Noah smiled before turning to face Freddie, who was standing behind them. 'Bye, Freddie.' Noah's innocent mind wasn't picking up on the negative vibes being thrown at him by the two women. Britney responded by giving them both a death glare.

Britney already knew Noah's easy friendship with Freddie and Isabelle was bound to get complicated in a couple of years, especially with the mums involved. She'd seen drips of the venom slipping in through the cracks not too long ago, when Freddie and Noah had their first fight and she had been called into school. Whatever happened in the future, she would always be in her son's corner.

She felt her phone vibrate in her pocket as they entered their flat.

Dylan: I need to talk to you. Please x

· · · · · · · · · ·

BRITNEY WAS NERVOUS. SHE didn't understand what he wanted to talk to her about. She knew things had shifted ever since that night when Dylan came round to comfort her after what happened with Noah. They had started texting again, but they had kept their distance. She knew exactly why. She was scared. Terrified of fully exposing herself to someone, all the different layers of her from the inside out—the good, the bad, and the ugly.

Something inside her had changed, though, when she saw Dylan's expression on the playground. She noticed how much lighter and more liberated his posture was. It was the first time she'd seen him without a trace of guilt or pain in his expression, and she was desperate to find out what had caused it.

Her anxiety was brought to the forefront when she heard a small knock on her front door. She walked over but paused for a moment before opening it. She had a feeling something big was about to happen. She could feel it in her bones, but she wasn't sure whether it was good or bad.

She opened the door and was greeted with Dylan's gentle smile. For a brief moment, silence descended as they both stood there, taking each other in. Then, finally, she took a step back, allowing him to enter. 'Do you want a drink?' she asked as she closed the door behind him.

'No, thanks. We need to talk,' he said as he took a step closer to her. 'We can't avoid it anymore.'

So he wanted to dive right into it. No small talk required. Her stomach clenched. She walked away from the door and into the living room, with him close behind her.

She turned to face him. 'I miss you.' Why would she say that? *STUPID. Stupid girl.*

'I miss you too. Everything has been such a mess. I know that. But I—' As he took her in, he paused. 'What's wrong? You're shaking,' he exclaimed.

'I'm fine,' she mumbled, embarrassed that her nerves had gotten the best of her yet again. *He missed her?*

'Are you sure?' he asked, leaning down.

'Yeah. Just cold, I guess.'

'Here.' He took off his hoodie and handed it to her.

'No. It's fine. Anyway, what were you saying?' She pushed it back towards him and sat down on the sofa.

He sat next to her, fiddling with his fingers before turning his head, his eyes softening when they landed on hers. 'I don't know how to do this. I don't even know where to start. I just know that we can't keep avoiding each other. Whatever this is, whatever we're attempting to accomplish, it isn't working.'

'What's not working?' she choked out. Where was he going with this? Was he leaving town? Was that what he was trying to tell her?

'I can't get you out of my head, and not seeing you, not being around you, is killing me. For the first time in five years, I can breathe again. When I'm around you.' His head sagged into his hands.

Her heart burst wide open. What did she say to that? Did she tell him that her heart had never beat for anyone the way it did for him? Did she tell him that he was going too far? No, she just sat there and stared.

'Please say something.' His voice cracked.

She realised she had to make a decision. What she said at that precise moment would either make or break them. She averted her gaze. She knew what she wanted, but was that enough to compel her to act?

'It's killing me, too,' she admitted.

He snapped his head up in response. The hope that flashed in his eyes made her let out a small gasp.

'I can't do this back and forth with you anymore,' he said. 'I feel for you. You know that. I've not done a very good job at hiding it, no matter how hard I've tried. I'm done fighting it. I want you. All of you.'

She wanted him too. She couldn't fight it anymore either. After everything she'd been through this year, she couldn't put herself through any more agony. 'I want you, too.'

He reached over and pulled her into his arms. His forehead touched hers. She saw it all—the love in his eyes. She had finally broken through his defences and, for the first time in her life, she could picture a future with someone. Her eyes welled up. It was all too much, what she was feeling, what she was finally allowing herself to feel. She could feel the soft pads of his thumbs wiping away the tears that had somehow escaped. She closed the gap between them and finally kissed him, fearful he'd pull away again. She wanted this, wanted him. He pulled back gently, but before she could react, he gazed into her eyes and placed his lips back onto hers. The kiss was gentle. Loving. Careful. Testing the waters.

She didn't want to test the waters anymore. She wanted to be free, and judging by the look in his eyes, he did as well. She didn't know what had happened to push him to this moment, what finally released him from the guilt and grief that had followed him around like a dark cloud. She would find that out later, but for now, she wanted to live in the moment with him. She pulled back and stood. He looked up at her in confusion before she extended her hand to him and glanced at her bedroom door. As he stood, his understanding shone through, and he placed his hand in hers.

Once they were inside her bedroom, she slowly stepped back and undressed. She didn't know what had come over her or why she was suddenly so confident with her body. He made her feel so comfortable and powerful, like the whole world was hers on which to make her mark. She approached him as he gazed down at her, taking his time in relishing the sight of her naked body in front of him. She grabbed his T-shirt and pulled it over his head before reaching for his jeans. He drew her into a desperate kiss as they both yanked his jeans and underwear down quickly.

As he gently placed her on the bed, his soft fingers caressed her most private spot, and the love she felt was liberating. Intoxicating. As he looked down at her, she could see it burning through his eyes. As he intimately touched her, her entire body caught fire. She leaned up and caught his lips in a soft kiss. He explored her mouth as he explored other parts of her body. She was so lost in the sensations that she almost missed him asking her if she was ready. She gave a slight nod as he cradled her face and kissed the tip of her nose, and she let out a hitched moan as he entered her.

His eyes glazed over as he slowly began to make love to her. The emotion there told her everything she needed to know. He adored her. The revelation made her heart sing. He leaned forward, cupped her face between his palms, and continued to kiss her. The pressure deep inside her was building. Her body begged for more. He groaned as she lifted her hips to meet his thrusts and quickly increased the pace. Her entire body trembled.

Her eyes were watering. She'd never felt anything like it before. Not just the pleasure, but the connection. Love. Trust. Passion. The bond they'd already had only intensified. He reached down and rubbed her softly as his hips sped up. 'I love you,' she whispered.

He froze inside her for a second and gazed into her eyes. Her heart burst at his expression. The emotion in his eyes. 'I love you too,' he whispered before he picked up the pace and pounded into her. That was enough for her entire body to spill over. The pleasure surged through her as she let out a loud gasp and experienced an orgasm like never before. His eyes flared at her reaction as she tightened around him, and he followed closely behind her.

She was flying. Her body and soul had never felt more in sync. She loved this man with everything in her and was no longer afraid to let him in. She couldn't help it if she tried. He knocked down every single wall she had built up over the years.

. . . . ● . ● . . . .

WHEN SHE RECEIVED A phone call the following day, her mood plummeted. It was the police, and they wanted her to come in for questioning.

Chapter Twenty-Three

THE INTERVIEWS

AT THE BAYNOR GREEN Police Station, Officer Sam Crucker sat at his small desk. As he read the file before him, he tried to remain calm. He wanted every piece of information he could get his hands on. Despite this, every lead he had seemed to come to a dead end. He slammed his pen on his desk and rubbed his face with his hand. Since he was assigned to this case seventy-two hours ago, the Hennering family and his boss had been on his arse nonstop. The Hennerings donated a lot of money to this station, so his boss wanted to prioritise this investigation.

Sam sighed and leaned over his work laptop, placing the file next to him. He put his headphones in his ears and began scanning through his most recent file of recorded interviews from the previous twenty-four hours.

Anna Hennering
Sarah Colling

Britney Adamson

He went to Adamson's first.

Sam: This interview is now being recorded. I am officer Sam Crucker from the Baynor Green Police Department. Also present is Officer Emilia Montgomery. There are no other persons present conducting this interview. This is an interview with ... state your full name, please.'

Britney: Britney Adamson.

Sam: Britney, please tell me the last time you saw or spoke with Ian Hennering.

Britney: The last time I saw him was three weeks ago, coming out of the corner shop on Wilner Street. I didn't speak to him. I don't even think he saw me. I glanced at him and walked in the opposite direction.

Sam: Okay, we have on file that you stated he attempted to kidnap your son from Rovon Moore Primary School on the fifteenth of last month, which was over two weeks ago.

Britney: Yes, and in that report, I stated that it was my mother, Melanie Adamson, who witnessed and stopped that from happening. That last time I saw Ian was a week before that happened. I haven't seen or spoken to him at all. To be honest, I haven't heard anything else about him since the incident I mentioned.

Sam clicked out of the interview and opened Sarah Colling's up. This time he skipped the recording forward, past the introductions, before playing it.

Sarah: The last time I saw or spoke to Ian was when I went to try to pick up some of his wife's stuff.

Sam: And when was that?

Sarah: Erm, the thirteenth.

Sam: Why were you picking up some of his wife's belongings?

Sarah: His wife had recently left him and was staying with me.

He paused the recording. He already knew what had allegedly happened between Ian and his wife, Anna, based on the interviews. He was required to write 'allegedly' on his report for legal reasons, but Sam was utterly convinced that Ian was an abusive son of a bitch. He clicked into Anna Hennering's recording and skimmed through it before pressing play.

Anna: After what he did to me, why wouldn't he just pick up and leave? He must have realised that I would eventually come here and spill everything about the toxic, abusive marriage I'm in.

Sam: I have to ask this so it's on file. Why didn't you speak up sooner about the alleged abuse you endured?

Anna: It's not ALLEGED! It happened. You want to see some bruising to prove it? It's been less than three weeks since I got away, and I've not entirely healed yet. (It was at this point in the interview when Anna stood and gently lifted the side of her shirt to reveal the purple bruising up her side.)

Sam: I'm sorry. I just have to ask these questions to rule out any involvement in his disappearance.

Sam stopped the recording and glanced over the other ones he had.

Dylan Colling
Melanie Adamson
Jill Hennering

None of them brought him any closer to solving this case. He wanted to bring in Ryker Colling for an interview. Ryker was well known in town, and given Ian's history with Sarah, he would have been an ideal candidate to bring in. Sam had attempted to add his name to the list, but someone much higher up kept removing it. He had no idea who it was, and he had tried to question it with his supervisor a couple of times in the last few days, but he kept getting knocked back.

He had a few loose ends to tie up, and he was expecting a phone call shortly. Once he had that information, he would be ready to submit his final report and findings to his supervisor and the Hennering family.

·•·•·•·•·•·

'MRS. HENNERING, THANK YOU for coming. Will your husband be able to join us?' Sam asked as he entered one of the station's small meeting rooms. Jill was already inside, seated on one of the padded chairs arranged around the glass table, her bobbed hair perfectly styled and a small designer handbag slung over her arm. Her posture was stiff as she looked at him, running her eyes up and down his torso before huffing slightly.

'No, he's at work. Do you have any news for me, or what?'

Sam tried so hard to maintain his calm demeanour, restraining himself from reacting to the snobbish woman. 'Yes, it appears that your son has emptied and closed his bank account. He sent his resignation letter to his employer through the post and after speaking to his wife, Anna, I believe he may have left town by his own free will.'

'My son would not leave town without telling me!'

'We have spoken to a large number of people. Your son appears to have a pattern of just upping and leaving without a word. He has done this before, hasn't he?'

'Yes but ... but ...' she stuttered.

'If I hear anything else or if any new evidence comes to light, then please bring it forward. But for the time being, I'm hoping he'll contact you soon once he's settled.'

'I still believe you're far too young to be working on my family's behalf. I don't trust pretty boys like you,' Jill said darkly before leaping from her seat and heading for the door.

After she was gone, Sam took a deep breath. He was thirty-six years old, but he appeared much younger with his dark brown eyes, long lashes, tanned skin, and full lips. His height made up for his youthful features—at a staggering six feet, three inches, he towered over many of his colleagues. Sam was used to people judging him based on his appearance. They automatically assumed that he had it easy and sailed through life. They didn't realise he grew up being tossed around different care homes after his mother died of a drug overdose when he was ten. He never knew his father. He worked hard to end up where he was today, and he was damn proud of it.

He had a meeting with his boss in a half hour to discuss his findings. Personally, he was sick of the Ian Hennerings of the world and how society lifted them up and made them feel superior to everyone else simply because they were born into money. He had more important cases to work on and better things to do than look for a rich, pampered prick who'd most likely split town as soon as things got rough for him. He would put this case to rest for the time being; however, a nagging voice in his head kept directing him to Ryker Colling. He ignored it for now and went along with his day.

Later that night, as he pulled into the parking lot of his two-bedroom apartment, he reflected on the interviews he had conducted over the previous few days. Anna's was the one that stood out the most in his mind. The redhead had been through a lot in such a short period of time:

her sister was killed in a car accident, she no longer had much contact with her family, her husband had been abusing her for years, and then she discovered he had a secret child she had no knowledge of.

Now she was here in Baynor Green, starting from scratch. He'd met a lot of different people in his personal and professional life who had been in similar or even worse situations, but for some reason, he couldn't get Anna out of his head. He wasn't sure if it was an inkling concerning the case or something personal.

Hopefully, Ian would contact his parents soon, and all this worrying would be for nothing.

· · · · • · • · · ·

WHEN SARAH ARRIVED AT work that day, the café was bustling as usual. As a result, she didn't have much time to talk to anyone and ask if they had heard anything from the police. She still hadn't heard a peep. She convinced herself that was good news. Then again, what if Ian came out of hiding—or from wherever he went—and tried to make their lives even more difficult? Sarah just hoped that wherever he was, he would stay there.

It was typical of Jill to blame her yet again when Ian decided to skip town. She thought Jill should be used to her son upping and leaving whenever things got tough. It was what he did best. After attempting to kidnap Noah, he must have known there was no way up from there, so he legged it. Good riddance. When the police called her in for questioning, she wasn't surprised at all that Jill would have put her at the top of her suspect list after the blow-up they had not too long ago in Sarah's apartment.

She was about to take another order when Keith burst into the café and nearly threw himself behind the window booth in the far corner. Sarah was about to storm over and ask him what the hell he was doing when Rosie Forrester walked through the door with a scowl on her face.

'I saw him come in here. Where is he?'

Sarah rolled her eyes. 'I don't know what's going on, but please don't bring your personal problems in here.'

'Whatever!' she said. 'You tell him to call me immediately. If he doesn't, I'll show up at his house every night this week until he does.' She stormed back out the café door, shooting Sarah a dirty look as she left.

Sarah laughed as she walked over to Keith's hiding spot. 'You can't hide from her forever, you know. I thought you two were all loved up, anyway.'

Keith eventually dragged himself out from behind the booth and stood to his full height. 'We were until she became possessive and told me she was leaving her husband and that I would have to give up my music to support her.' He scoffed. 'We haven't even been seeing each other for that long, and I told her from the beginning it will never be anything serious. I mean, she's married, for fuck's sake. So obviously, I ended it there and then. I told her we wanted different things. Ever since, she's been trying to call and message me. So I blocked the crazy bint. So now she's resorted to chasing me down the street whenever she sees me!'

'It's your own fault for getting involved with a married woman in the first place. Just don't bring your shit in here.' Sarah rolled her eyes. 'I can't afford to lose customers because you don't keep your dick in your pants.'

'Yeah, yeah,' Keith sighed as he approached the counter to order himself a drink.

After a couple of hours, Sarah decided to take a quick break. It was quieting down, and her feet were killing her. She sat in the nearest empty booth and scanned through her phone. Jake was on his way and should be here any minute now.

'Sis, what's all this I'm hearing about the police taking you in for questioning?' Ryker asked as he interrupted her scrolling and sat opposite her. She hadn't even noticed him walking in.

'How did you hear about that?'

'Brooke told me. So, what happened? What did they wanna know?' he asked in a bored tone as he flicked his eyes over his phone.

Since when did he and Brooke have private conversations?

'Well, after Jill and I had that blow-up at my apartment, she went running to the police about Ian going missing, and of course, the first person she blames is me,' Sarah scoffed.

'Missing? That useless wanker most likely ran off with the nearest slag he could find.' Ryker chuckled.

'That's exactly what I thought, but that's not the thing I'm worried about.'

'Why, what's up?' he asked as he leaned back and rested his head on the booth.

'Jake,' Sarah mumbled.

'What's up with you now? I thought you and Jake were all loved up again,' Ryker said as he checked his phone yet again. She wondered what was so interesting with the way he was glued to it today. It wasn't like him at all.

She quickly looked around the café and noticed one of Ryker's acquaintances glancing over at them with a curious expression on his face. She ignored it for the time being.

'I'm just worried. What if Jake wants to go back to London? My life is here! I want to stay here. Then what if once he gets back down there, he—'

'Jake is not our prick of a sperm donor, and you know that. It would help if you stopped letting your insecurities take over,' he said with a stern look.

He was right. She loved Jake, and she knew he loved her. He wasn't her father. She exhaled loudly and finally let that worry wash away.

'You're right,' she said, smiling.

'Besides.' Ryker snorted and jerked his thumb behind his back. 'Do you think that whipped fucker will be able to even attempt to force you to do anything you don't want to do?'

Sarah followed his gesture. Jake had just walked into the café and immediately helped Brooke carry a couple of cups over to a table for a customer. He turned to face them and smiled at Sarah.

'Fuck's sake, are his balls shoved in your purse too?' Ryker muttered in disbelief as he rolled his eyes and looked around the room. 'What?' he barked at the nosy man Sarah had noticed earlier—one of Ryker's acquaintances, she'd guessed—constantly looking over at them.

The man's eyes widened. 'You've been walking funny today.'

'What business is it of yours? Piss off. I could still handle you if that's what you're aiming for,' Ryker erupted in rage.

The man's face blanched as he averted his gaze.

'The cheek of these pricks thinking because I pulled my back out lifting something heavy, I still couldn't handle the whole lot of them,' Ryker growled.

'What is wrong with you today, anyway? You're moody as fuck and glued to your phone more than usual.'

'I had some serious business to take care of, that's all. So anyway, I've got to head out.' He jumped up and walked out of the café without saying goodbye or even looking back.

Jake came running over, grinning as he leaned down and kissed her on the lips. 'Hey, you.'

The rest of her shift flew by, and she went home with Jake that night. The only thing that seemed out of the ordinary were Brooke's constant questions about Ryker and how he was doing. Sarah found it extremely odd.

Chapter Twenty-Four

THE RESOLUTION

BEEP, BEEP.

BRITNEY SIGHED and slowly opened her eyes. A text message alert on her phone had jolted her out of her slumber. She knew she should have put her phone on silent last night, but out of habit, she'd left it on loud. She wondered if there had been any news from the police, or if they had at the very least removed her from their suspect list. She wanted Ian to pay for what he'd done, but in the right way. She wanted him in jail, and with him disappearing again, it didn't leave her with much hope. She was sure he'd be halfway across the country, if not in another country entirely, by now.

When she reached for her phone, she discovered two new texts waiting for her. She started with the first one.

Dylan: Morning. Want to do something today, the three of us? x

She grinned as she replied.

Britney: Sure. I'll call you soon. X

She closed the message and opened the second message that had woke her up a couple of minutes ago.

Sarah: U & D Café Now x

Britney had told Sarah the day before that she was taking it easy today with it being a Sunday, which meant no school for Noah.

She immediately called Dylan.

'Hey, I just got a text from Sarah, telling us to meet her at the café ASAP. What's going on?' she asked as soon as he answered.

'No clue. Something to do with Ian, I think.'

Britney groaned. She hoped like hell that he hadn't shown back up. 'Wanna meet there, or—?'

'I'll come yours, and we can walk over together.'

'Okay, I'll get Noah ready. See you soon.'

She hung up the phone and dragged herself out of bed. She was not a morning person at all.

Her thoughts returned to Sarah, and she wondered what Ian had done now. She hoped there wouldn't be any more bad news. She'd had her fair share of bad luck this year, but there had also been a lot of good for both her and Noah. She hurriedly dressed and went to get Noah ready for the day.

· · · ● · ● · · · ·

THE CAFE WAS UNUSUALLY quiet that morning, given that Sunday was usually one of its busiest days. Noah came bombarding into the café first, trailed by a red-cheeked—due to the frosty early-December weather—out-of-breath Britney and a laughing Dylan.

'Slow down. Stop running before you fall and hurt yourself,' Britney shrieked as she reached to grab his hand.

'Sorry, Mummy!' Noah giggled. He was dressed in an oversized black coat with a woolly winter hat.

'He's just excited. You know what the town gets like around this time of year,' Dylan defended with a chuckle.

Britney responded with a smile. She looked around the café until her gaze stopped on her source. Sarah sat in a small booth at the back of the room, accompanied by Jake, Anna, and Brooke.

'Over there,' Britney said to Dylan as they approached the booth.

Noah dashed ahead before coming to a halt at the foot of the table, exclaiming happily, 'SARAH!' He'd been in with Britney a few times in the last few weeks and had really taken to Sarah.

'Hello, sweetie. Do you want some chocolate-chip pancakes?' As Sarah scooted out of the booth and stood, she smiled down at Noah.

'CHOCO PAN—yes, please!' Noah jumped up and down in excitement. He was a big fan of chocolate pancakes, but Britney made sure she didn't make them too often so when he did get them, he saw them as a treat rather than an everyday occurrence.

'Morning, Sarah,' Britney uttered in an exhausted tone. After all, she had just spent the last twenty minutes chasing Noah across town.

'Well, don't you look a treat this morning?' Sarah laughed in response to Britney's messy winter hair and red cheeks from the cold that hadn't faded yet.

Britney responded with a playful roll of her eyes.

'Becky, will you bring Noah some chocolate-chip pancakes, please?' Sarah cocked her head slightly to one of the young waitresses on duty passing the table.

'Sure,' Becky responded by looking down and smiling at Noah. He immediately looked down shyly, and his cheeks heated up in response. It was the sweetest thing ever. Noah wasn't usually shy around new people.

'Who is that, Mummy?' he asked, still staring at the floor and nervously moving from side to side.

'That's one of the waitresses who works for Sarah.'

'Oh, she's pretty.' He giggled shyly.

Britney's heart burst. How sweet—his first little crush.

'So, what have you got us all here before eight on a Sunday morning for?' Dylan yawned as he slid into the booth beside Anna.

'Well, Anna saw Jill in the supermarket last night with a face like thunder,' Sarah said. 'She overheard her complaining to one of her friends about how the police in this town don't do their job properly and that instead of finding out where Ian is, they simply closed the case and informed her that he had left town on his own accord, based on the evidence they had gathered.'

'So that means he's really gone, and we won't be getting dragged into the station again anytime soon?' Britney interrupted in a hopeful tone.

'That's exactly what it means ... and just in time for Christmas too.'

'We should still keep a lookout, though. He could just be hiding out, waiting to strike back,' Anna mumbled, a worried expression on her face.

'Let's not think about that. I think we should just try to put it all behind us,' Brooke jumped in for the first time since Britney arrived.

'You're right!' Sarah sighed before she glanced towards Anna. 'Try not to worry so much. Think of it this way: if he does show back up, it will be all over town, especially with his family getting the police involved. There is no way he would even attempt to come at you now that he's in the spotlight. In my opinion, this is the first good thing Jill has ever done.' Sarah snorted.

'I'm just glad that Dickhead is out of the picture. I don't give a shit what happened to him,' Jake said.

'Agreed.' Dylan nodded.

'Anyway, Anna, that bitch Jill has your dog. We need a dognapping plan in place, pronto,' Brooke stated.

'What's this group meeting about? And why wasn't I invited?' Ryker teased as he slid into the booth next to Brooke, who immediately moved over to make room for him.

'Where did you come from?' Sarah asked.

'I walked in while you were all huddled together like you were planning a heist. So again, what's all this about?'

'Sarah was just explaining how the case of Ian's disappearance has been dropped,' Dylan explained.

'Good. So what are you all carrying on for? Move on, already.' Ryker rolled his eyes as he took a sip of Brooke's coffee.

'Get your own!' Brooke snapped as she reached over to reclaim her cup from him.

Ryker swatted her hands away before continuing. 'Ian most likely ran off with some random slag. Why is everyone making such a huge deal about this? He's gone. End of story. Now, I'm starving. Who's getting breakfast in?'

'Ryker's right. I get that Ian's hurt you all, but we should just be thankful that he's gone,' Brooke sighed.

'Short stuff, you finally agree with me. I'll have to note this time and date.' Ryker laughed.

'Chocolate pancakes!' Becky interrupted with a plate for Noah in her hands.

As the plate was placed in front of him, his little eyes lit up. He dove right in and had chocolate sauce all over his face within ten seconds. Everyone laughed at the sight, except for Britney.

'You aren't the ones who will have to clean up all this mess when he's finished,' Britney groaned, making the others laugh even harder.

'It's nearly Christmas. Let's leave all the Ian shit in the past unless something else happens. Clear?' Ryker said.

Everyone turned to look at each other before turning back to Ryker. 'Clear,' they all said at once.

· · • • • • • • · ·

SAM WALKED OUT OF a small takeout place after a long day at work. There was no way he was cooking tonight. He was due back in the station at seven a.m., and all he wanted to do was get home, put his feet up, and enjoy a cold beer in front of the TV. Nicola, one of the women he worked with at the station, had been flirting with him since he began. He'd made it clear that he didn't want to mix business and pleasure, but that didn't stop her from trying. She'd invited him to join her for a drink after his shift. Of course, he'd declined politely. He didn't need to be making any enemies at the station.

As he turned a street corner, heading towards his home, he slammed straight into someone.

'I'm so sorry, I wasn't watching where I was going,' a soft voice said.

Sam immediately recognised the long red hair and green eyes. Anna Hennering, walking a small Yorkshire terrier. *I didn't know she had a dog.*

'It's okay. I didn't see you either.' He laughed awkwardly. The last time he saw her, he was questioning her about her husband's disappearance.

'Officer Crucker?' she asked with a smile.

'Call me Sam.' He grinned.

'I didn't know you lived around here.'

'Yeah, just a couple of streets over ... speaking of, I best get going before this goes cold,' he said as he lifted his takeaway bag up.

'Oh, okay. It was nice to see you again.' She paused. 'Under different circumstances, of course.'

'Of course. Hopefully I'll see you around again soon.'

'Bye. Come on, Maisy!' she said before she hurried off in the opposite direction.

Sam watched her go before he carried on with his short walk home. She was attractive. He would admit that to himself, but he would never do anything about it. He'd interviewed her not too long about her husband's disappearance, for fuck's sake. He wasn't an idiot. The one thing he had always done—and done very well, he might add—was never mix his personal life with his professional one. Over the years, he had seen far too many fallouts with his colleagues to know the outcome of that.

Chapter Twenty-Five

THE TRUTH

CHRISTMAS WAS THE MOST talked-about month of the year in Baynor Green. The streets were lined with elaborate Christmas lights and illuminations that gleamed with pride. It was the middle of December, and as usual, the town had gone crazy for the holiday season. The annual unveiling of the large Christmas tree, smack dab in the middle of town, would take place the following week on Christmas Eve.

It was a tradition that Sarah cherished, not only because she loved Christmas, but also because it was the only time of year when both sides of town came together to hear the local high school choir sing 'Silent Night.' The two sides wouldn't interact much, but standing side by side as a community was, in Sarah's opinion, a step in the right direction. Of course, there was still a lot of work to be done, but it gave her hope for the town's future.

Now, however, she was rushing towards the café, Anna close behind. Jake had texted her that he needed to see her right away and to bring

Anna with her. She panicked, wondering what could have possibly happened now. This last year had been the most bizarre and unexpected of her life, from opening her business to her friendship with Britney to the rekindling of her relationship with Jake, the fallout with her parents, Ian's return and subsequent disappearance, and her developing friendship with Anna.

Once she got closer, she noticed that the front of the café was dark. It was the middle of the day. Where was everyone? Brooke was supposed to open up that morning. Sarah approached the front door and noticed it was open. *What was going on?*

She walked into the dark room and noticed Jake standing in the middle of it, candlelight lighting up the room as all the tables behind him were covered with candles. The first thing that came to mind was that she was thankful she had insurance, in case of an accident.

'What's going on?' she asked.

'I remember the first time I saw you. We were four years old, and you were running around the nursery playground. Not a lot interested me at the time if it didn't involve playtime or superheroes, but you stood out to me for some reason. I didn't understand it. I mean, you were just a yucky girl.' He laughed. 'When we were six, your next-door neighbour got married, and you had it in your head at the time that you needed a husband then and there. So we got married under the slides at the park. It wasn't a very long marriage, as you claimed we were *'vorced'* a couple of weeks later, after I broke your crayon in class. Over the years, we were each other's first kiss, first time ... you're the only person I've ever truly loved. Leaving you was the hardest thing I have ever had to do in my entire life. I never want to be without you again.' He inhaled deeply, nervously.

Sarah's eyes welled up with tears, and her heart burst. The love she felt for this man was undeniable.

He approached her, got down on one knee, and reached into his pocket.

'I love you. I want to be with you for the rest of my life.' He pulled a small black box from his pocket and opened it in front of her. When she saw the stunning ring he had chosen, the butterflies in her stomach exploded. 'Will you marry me?' he whispered.

'Of course I will!'

He leapt to his feet and placed the ring on her finger before lifting her and spinning her around. 'Come out! Come out! She said YES!'

Suddenly, the lights came on, and a large crowd cheered as they emerged from the kitchen door. Ryker, Brooke, Dylan, Britney, Noah, some of the girls who worked for her, Pete and Mark, Keith, a couple of the guys from The Blue Bell, and a few of Ryker's goons were among them.

'It's about time. It took you almost twenty-four years.' Ryker smirked as he slapped Jake on the back playfully.

'Oh, ha ha. Prick!' Jake chuckled as he rolled his eyes.

'I'm so happy for you!' Brooke squealed in excitement as she ran towards Sarah and pulled her into a hug.

'Congratulations.' Britney smiled as she walked up to her with Dylan in tow.

'You deserve all the happiness in the world.' Dylan smiled as he pulled her towards him.

As other people congratulated her, Sarah reached for Jake's hand. He was her future. This place, all these people, were her happy place, and nothing could ever change that. These people, right here, were her family.

· · · ◆ · ◆ · · ·

AS BRITNEY SAT IN the café surrounded by the large celebrating group, she smiled. For the first time in her life, she had people who truly cared about her. She was finally excited about what the future had in store for her. She cast a glance over at Dylan, who was standing at the counter, getting drinks for them while holding a giggling Noah in his arms so he could see over it. Dylan turned and caught her eye, giving her a slight grin before turning back to pay for their drinks.

She took a look around the room. Sarah was laughing with Jake and a small group of people by one of the window booths. Brooke stood off to the side, a worried expression on her face—Britney made a mental note to check on her later—as Ryker spoke with her.

'Mummy!' Noah dashed over and threw himself into her arms.

Britney laughed as she hugged him back and looked up to see Dylan approaching with their drinks.

'Here you go,' he said, setting her glass of lemonade on the table next to her and handing Noah his orange juice bottle.

'Thank you,' Noah said with a big grin on his face.

'You're welcome.' Dylan smiled, slightly ruffling his hair.

A loud shriek cut them off as they turned to look over at a father swinging his son around playfully as they laughed together.

Noah lowered his gaze to his orange juice, a thoughtful expression on his face. 'Mummy,' he murmured.

Britney knelt in front of him. 'Yes?'

'Is Mr. Coll your special friend?'

'I ... yes, he is,' she replied nervously. She wasn't expecting him to bring this up here, of all places.

'Does that mean ... he won't go away as my first daddy did?'

Britney's heart sank to the pit of her stomach as she gazed down at her child's innocent face. She could never understand how anyone could not love this adorable boy, or even want him to exist.

'Listen to me. I will always be here for you. You know that, right? You can always come to me for anything,' Dylan interrupted as he crouched next to her in front of Noah.

'I know,' Noah said softly before leaning in towards Dylan and murmuring, 'Daddy.'

Tears sprung to Britney's eyes. *I will not cry ... oh, who am I kidding?* Tears streamed down her cheeks as she noticed Dylan's own eyes filling up.

'Always, little man,' he said as he drew Noah into a hug.

'Dylan, Britney, get over here!' Sarah yelled from across the room, beckoning them over.

For the first time in her life, Britney felt confident meeting new people. They walked over to Sarah and the group of people surrounding her.

· · • • • • • • · ·

BROOKE WAS TREMBLING. SHE took deep breaths, but the memories continued to flood back to her. She felt sick. How was she supposed to deal with this? Carry on as if nothing happened? As if she didn't ... *no, don't go there.* Her stomach clenched. Could she keep lying like this?

'Stop thinking about it,' Ryker whispered in her ear as he stood behind her, gently placing his hands on her shoulders to comfort her.

'I can't. What if someone finds out? What if—'

'They won't. I took care of it,' he said, cutting her off.

'I know you did. I didn't know who else to turn to. I know we don't have the best relationship, but I didn't know anyone else who could deal with—'

'I know! I know. Calm down. No one is ever gonna find out. As far as everyone else is concerned, he fucked off with a load of cash. Trust me. I know what I'm doing. You have nothing to be worried about,' he sighed softly, running his thumbs over her shoulders.

'But what I did—'

'You can't stay hidden for long...' Ian's deep voice chuckled.

Ian was stumbling out of The Blue Bells when he saw her walking home late at night and decided to harass her in one of his drunken states. One, because he enjoyed picking on people who were weaker than him, and two, to retaliate against Sarah. Brooke told him to fuck off and ran home, unaware that he had followed her until it was too late.

Brooke was hiding in the wardrobe, terrified. She banged her left foot hard, looked down to see what it was, and immediately saw an old bat that Ryker had given to her when she was twelve – when she was chased home by a bunch of lads she went to school with who wanted to scare the fat girl – and she kept it hidden out of the way – not that she would ever tell anyone, especially Ryker. She was grateful for it right now. She picked it up, eager to put it to use.

'It was self-defence,' Ryker said. 'He broke into your home and attacked you. If you didn't still have that bat I gave you when we were kids, he would have finished the job. You know that. It wasn't your fault. You just wanted to stop him.' He glanced around quickly, making sure no one was looking their way or listening in on their conversation. He felt protective of her. In a way, he always had been. He could count on one hand whom he felt protective of, and all of them were his blood—except this little spitfire who stood in front of him.

He was glad she'd called him that night. Once he'd gotten to her apartment and saw the mess, he jumped right into action. This wasn't his first time covering up a crime scene, and it certainly wouldn't be his last. He made sure there were no traces of that bastard left, nothing that would link him to Brooke. After she explained what had occurred, Ryker was glad that the fucker was dead because if he were still alive, he would have hunted him down and finished the job himself.

All that mattered was that he was gone, and she was still here. He was grateful for the bat he'd given her when they were twelve, and he was glad she'd kept it because if she hadn't, instead of celebrating an engagement, they would all be attending her funeral right now.

The End

Afterword

THANK YOU

THANK YOU SO MUCH for reading The Divide. I hope you loved reading Sarah and Britney's story just as much as I loved writing it. Please make sure to leave a review on Amazon, Goodreads , and Bookbub.
Follow me on social media and be the first to receive exclusive content, updates on upcoming books, giveaways, and specials; Instagram , Facebook
Join the Dark Confessions Of Baynor Green Facebook Group
Join my ARC team and get my future books for free and before everyone else.

Acknowledgments

TO MY INCREDIBLE PARTNER, who has been a rock for me throughout this journey. He has helped me so much in gaining my confidence and pursuing my dream.

Thank you to all of my friends and family, especially my father, for your love and support over the years.

Thank you so much to all of the amazing writers I've met along the way, as well as everyone in this community who has been so supportive.

Thank you to everyone who has helped make this dream a reality.

Printed in Great Britain
by Amazon

83049815R00148